Take the Highway

a novel by

ELEN GHULAM

ISBN: 978-0-9781872-5-5

www.ihath.com

For Yusuf Hassan

When I pass through your name.

I feel like somebody from Damascus that is passing through
Andalucía.

Lonely with my breath.

Here is where the lemons lit up for you the salt of my blood.

Over here.

Right here.

Is where the wind fell off my horse

When I pass through your name.

There is no army holding a siege.

No country.

As if I am the last of the guards.

Or a poet taking a leisurely walk through his poem.

In Damascus, the sky walks along roads

barefoot

and barefoot.

Inspiration, rhyme and rhythm

are rendered useless

--- Excerpt from a poem by Mahmoud Darwish

Multi Media Pack

To receive multi-media content (videos, stories, music, coloring pages and much more) related to this novel, subscribe to the Take The Highway mailing list here:

ihath.com/MailingList/?p=subscribe&id=6

You will receive ten emails over nine weeks.

Ignition

YES!

Yes yes yes yes yes yes yes.

One yes tumbling down the hill following the other. Erupting like lava from the depths of yesness. Little yeses, large yeses, purple, pink and lilac yeses. All possible future utterances of yes and all past yes thoughts that have been suppressed by pre-historic humans are colliding, right this minute, inside my chest. If I was a novelist I would write a whole book with nothing but the word yes repeated in different languages and styles. Imagine curling up in bed with a book at night, a warm cup of camomile tea in hand, opening a random page to read: Yes na'am aywa ci ano oui aye ken yah yep not-no. A more creative writer would find a way to make the string of yeses tell a story. If I was a visual artist I would create a giant yes

1

sculpture from random objects. Macaroni, garbage, discarded electronics, clothing, shoes, yarn, whoopee cushions, Campbell's soup cans, jewelry, a David Bowie poster, a fork, chips of wood, my favorite book, human hair, a snow globe, a clown's nose, a light bulb and a piece of rock from the Berlin wall—all glued together to spell out yes. Even after I finished authoring the Yes book and building the Yes sculpture, I would still not be able to express this Yes! I'm feeling right now—Yes! this car ride is the best drive in the whole damn world. This is not a human body directing a vehicle, this is the history of yesness colliding into a single intense experience inside my imagination.

Yes! I am day dreaming.

My hands are loosely holding the black leather steering wheel—caressing, really. I am driving down an empty curvy road. The car swerves right and then it swerves left. With ease. I am in command. The blueness in the sky kisses the green tops of trees in the horizon. My favorite song is on the radio. Since there is nobody around I feel comfortable as I sing along. A traffic sign appears in the distance. I can't read what it says. A few blissful twists and turns in the road follow. At last, I can decipher the words: "Get Back To Your Date" instructs the neon yellow lettering on corrugated aluminum. What an odd traffic sign? ... Oh, right! I have to hurry up and get back to my date. Sheesh! I forgot! I am on a date with Steve. I hit the brakes, park the car on the side of the road and turn off the engine. I should stop day dreaming and pay attention to Steve. I swallow the drool pooling in my mouth and begin looking

at my date's lips, hoping to unlock the words billowing out of his mouth.

This is our first date. We met through iDate.com—an online dating site. After exchanging a few e-nudges and emails, Steve suggested that we meet for a cup of coffee. He chose this place. It's called Ram Blast Coffee. It has wooden panels for walls, wooden floors and a wooden counter, table and chairs. It looks rustic and cozy. Steve gets a brownie point simply for bringing me here. Definitely will be willing to go on a second date with this dude. Steve has thin pale lips, his hair line looks like it might start receding as we speak. He is wearing a tweed sweater and right this minute he is telling me about a hockey match he watched recently. At least I think it's hockey. Maybe it's football. My poor brain has been finely trained to tune out when somebody begins to talk about sports. All I hear is blah blah blah blah and then blah passed blah blah blah blah. I notice Steve's hand gestures and body language. At least he is displaying a kind of passion for something. Passion is good. He doesn't seem that interesting, or even funny, but at least he is not like the last Steve I met, who spent the whole date talking about the revolutionary health benefits of flax seed. Or the Steve before him who brought his three self-published books about how big corporations are corrupting the human soul, expecting me to purchase them. This Steve seems normal in comparison.

This business of finding a soul mate, or life partner or somebody to hang out with or whatever it is dating is supposed to result in, must be hard for men as well. I have a simple dating system in place. I schedule first dates every Tuesday and Thursday

where I meet potentials. I tried doing more but found that I was getting tired and confused about whom I was meeting when. If the initial encounter is not horrid, I schedule a second date for Friday or Saturday. This dating business is a part-time job. It takes so much effort to organize. Between my job as a technical writer at a software company and meeting single men, I hardly have time for anything else. I sometimes wonder what I will do with all the spare time once I am in a long term relationship. I will have to develop a hobby. Or who knows? Maybe I will have a couple of kids and busy myself with the dreary task of mothering. I will worry about that once I get to it. Right now, I am focusing on how Steve is moving his hands while keeping the fantastic car ride out of my mind. Oh, the sacrifices we women make for our love lives. Steve stopped talking, drew a quiet breath and then asked "So, Car, tell me about one of your dreams." A man who takes interest in his date's dreams! This is so unusual that I am caught unprepared. I don't know what to say. I am feeling more and more positive about this Steve. This Steve is a Yes!

Nameplate

MY NAME IS Car and one of my dreams is to drive my very own brand-new Nissan Juke. I don't want you to think that I am shallow. Loftier ambitions zip through the highway of my imagination. I am just starting with safest route for this "get to know me session". This unique ride features prominent wheel arches and a body high waistline which contrasts with the slim side windows, giving it a quirky look—a style that is unapologetically authentic without attempting to draw attention to itself. Unlike the beetle which says: "My grandparents thought this was cool and so now I am rebelling against my parents by driving the new retro car." It's not like a Porsche which says: "I am frantic for your noticing." No, no, no the Juke is sporty, strong and distinctive without any frills. And it comes in my favorite color—pistachio green. Some people say it

looks like a bug, but I think the Nissan Juke looks like a frog. A beautiful frog that is strong and self-confident and sits on a lotus leaf wisely observing the cacophony of activity around him and blinking gently every once in a while. The other bugs, fishes and birds don't pay him much attention. What they don't know is that their frog is the single living creature who has figured out the meaning of life and one day somebody will ask him the right question. The mystery that has puzzled all creation will be placed in plain view for all to see. I don't want you to think that my Juke is a frog that will alchemise into a prince charming if I were to bestow a warm wet kiss onto his slimy existence. Given the popular portrayal of frogs in our fairy-tales, I feel compelled to clarify this so as not to cause any confusion. I have money saved up in the bank and my features selected. Yes to moon-roof, no to built-in navigation. There is just one eensy weensy little problem preventing me from fulfilling this dream—I haven't managed to pass my driving test yet. So far, I have failed at this rudimentary passage into adulthood 16 times. I do know how to drive. In fact, I am a fantastic driver. I have spent thousands and perhaps even tens of thousands of dollars on driving lessons over the years. Something happens to me when the examiner sits next to me in the car with his big clipboard. A giant spaghetti monster of nerves attacks me and my body begins to shake, my perception of reality gets altered and even my vision gets all fuzzy. I have driven into a wall, straight onto a roundabout, passed a red light and even once grabbed the knee of the examiner in a fit of panic while avoiding crashing into a group of school children crossing the road. The poor examiner in that last stated

embarrassment looked terrified. I don't know if he was more afraid of sexual harassment or death. Disasters only happen to me during the test. The minute I receive my failure papers I am fit to drive safely again. My driving instructor, David, keeps telling me that I don't need any more driving lessons, that I just need to figure out a way to get over the nerves. I reply that I am trying to break the Guinness world record for most driving tests failed. So instead of riding in my pistachio green dream to work every morning, listening to my Tom Cochrane CD and fixing my lipstick in my mirror at a red light, I am forced to endure the tediousness of public transport.

The thing is, riding the bus every day is an unwelcome adventure waiting to happen. You never know who you will meet or end up sitting next to on a bus. Normally, I like a good escapade. Once in while it would be nice to turn off the bus drive movie and watch some lovely comedy about a heroine who gets everything that her heart desires instead. I would like to choose the DVD. On a bus the entertainment is chosen for me. I like having a choice ... that is all.

I wish we had met two years ago, or even a year ago. You would have encountered my original self. That would help you be more forgiving of my current state. I wouldn't say I was a happy person, as in being one of those annoying people that radiate

positivity and optimism like high beams on a dark country side road. People the likes of which we all wish would get hit by a bus. However, I had a bedrock of contentment that carried my weight. I never noticed it until it cracked beneath my feet. I sunk into the sludge. My moods swung up and down around a preprogrammed median. And then the great hand in the sky turned the knob down to a lower setting. In this new configuration I am not fun to be around. If I am to be honest, I myself no longer enjoy my own company. Therefore, I would be surprised if you found the ride we are about to take together pleasing. As it happens I am going through a heartbreak. As cliched as it sounds, "The One" that was supposed to last forever is no longer around. When heartbreak comes upon you, it's like you have been abducted in your sleep by a hydraulic claw crane truck, dumped in a car and left in a strange new city designed for people with your condition. You have no map and no navigation system. You must find your way out of this maze through trial and error by driving around wherever your wheels will take you. The fear of being stuck forever in this strange place is a definite reality.

Allow me to be your guide on a typical drive through heartbreak city. First you must visit denial square, where you must admire the Everything Is Fine statue. It was built by a brilliant artist who created it out of clear glass to make it invisible. I would be happy to describe what it looks like except I am yet to see it. I've been told by others that it is there. Take a right on Despair Avenue towards the Endless Junk Food Roundabout. There you shall circle so many times that you lose count. It has been scientifically proven

that eating ice-cream, chocolate and potato chips is effective in reducing the emotional distress caused by heartbreak. To help you with the self-loathing that will follow this overindulgence, you will exit the roundabout to take a dip in the Netflix Binge Watching pool. The instant gratification you will experience from watching sappy shows will make you almost forget where you are. Almost being the keyword. You can never outdrive a heartbreak. Once your exercise is done—yes, laying on the couch while watching Downton Abbey is exercise—you will continue for a visit to the Everything I Did Wrong Museum where you shall remind yourself of all your shortcomings. That wrong turn of phrase that led to a misunderstanding. The wardrobe malfunction at the office Christmas party. All the times you weren't your best and most beautiful self. To conclude the educational part of the day, you shall plunge into the Self Hatred Roundabout. Circling once shall suffice at this juncture. A single dose of staring into the dark abyss of your soul will last you for 24 hours. Finally, when you are dizzy and nauseous from all the circling you shall exit the roundabout and head towards the Stalking Bush, there you shall obsess over every tweet and facebook post your ex has made since your breakup. Fortunately, nobody knows that you are doing this, so you come across as sane to the non-residents of this city. You will see the picture of the new keychain that your ex has purchased and infer that he must have discarded the jade and silver keychain you bought for his birthday. This will trigger a trip to Seething Anger Bay. Along these shores you will remember all the mean things your ex has done and said over the years. You won't be able to contain your

rage and so you will pick up a stone to throw it into the sea. This will disturb all the sea creatures and they will swim to the surface to mock you. The crab, the fish and the octopus shall emerge to point a finger at you and laugh at your idiocy. The embarrassment will force you to get back into your car and drive over Despair Bridge. And for a moment you will think: "Yes! A Bridge! Surely this is the exit from this horrendous Heartbreak City!" but you are wrong. No matter what you do you will find yourself doing a U-turn and driving back into the dark heart of the city you are yearning to leave. Surely there must a way to exit this place? But so far you haven't found it.

I don't like anything in this city. I don't even like myself in it. Well! At least I haven't lost my sense of humor. So I guess there is one thing I do like. Hopefully I won't lose it in this horrid locale.

Patience.

My friend Stephanie says that I need to learn patience. For there are no short cuts and no efficient ways to get through this.

I have many great qualities and patience is not one of them. I face life's challenges head on and straight ahead. A no-nonsense approach is my favourite approach. Just get on with it. I have no time for wallowing in self pity. No patience for bemoaning the unfairness of this world. "Who cares? It is what it is and you just need to deal with it. Get on with it. Snap out of it. Do what needs to get done." I usually tell myself. But standing here, in this endless pool of sorrow with no solid ground in sight, none of my usual tricks seems to be working. The harder I work the more sadness I generate. Stephanie told me that I need to read "The Power of Now"

by Eckhart Tolle. I told her my power of now is "I want it now, right away, all at once." She laughed at my foolishness and said:" that is exactly why you need to read the book". I am extremely skeptical of self-help books. I don't need to read a book, I just need to use my common sense. There has to be an exit from heartbreak city. There just has to be.

I refuse to learn patience. It's just not me. Patience is not my personality. I hate waiting, even for the bus, even waiting in line at the supermarket. I am determined that this experience will not ruin my essence and teach me patience. I guess I am stubborn that way. Patience is for people who have nothing better to do. Why wait for stuff when you can run out and grab it? *Yalla, yalla, andele, andele,* come on and hurry up and get on with it. I want to snap my fingers to hurry things up. I am standing and fidgeting. Shifting my weight from one foot to the other. I am looking at my watch. I am biting my lower lip. Pulling at my hair. Tapping one foot, the other foot, then tapping my fingers. Are there any other impatient gestures that I can make? Perhaps I should jump up and down. Maybe I should kick some object. Perhaps there is some secret impatient gesture that I don't know about. I might try dancing the macarena in my imaginary car.

I have been plowing through this city for ages. But I am no longer lost in it. I have visited every nook and cranny at least once. I have driven across every street and road. Visited each house and monument. Walked in the parks and admired the vistas. It's high time to find the exit.

Sigh!

Today, I had a first date with Yuri in a swanky bar. He is hot. Even hotter than his profile picture on ItTakesTwo.com. He looks like a flesh and blood version of a Ken doll. Light brown hair, blue eyes like glacier lagoons, slim, athletic and perfect skin. He was wearing an expensive looking suit with a blue cotton shirt and no tie. A golden chain peeked through the opened shirt. It made me wonder what else would I find under that shirt. Yuri didn't waste time. Five minutes into our conversation he told me what he would like to do to me in bed. Normally, I would find that vulgar on a first date but from him it was turning me on. I felt myself swooning. I bet this guy gets away with murder on account of his looks. "Don't go to bed with him on a first date. Don't go to bed with him on first date. Don't go to bed with him on first date." I kept telling myself. It took enormous self discipline to say goodnight to Yuri and walk out of the bar on my own. I went home feeling extremely horny. Yuri is a yes. A definite candidate for a second date. Perhaps Yuri is my ticket to an exit from heartbreak city. Life as a single woman is starting to brighten. Oh the fun that is to be had!

I will not learn patience.

Fender Bender

I CAN'T BELIEVE what happened to me today. I was standing at the same bus stop where I usually wait for my ride home after work. Imagine a four lane street that is open only to buses and taxis in the heart of the downtown core of my beloved city. Pedestrians up the ying yang. So many people milling about that you could encounter your own brother and not notice him. The same familiar faces were standing around looking anxious to get to their destinations. I noticed a man walking towards me with an intense gaze. He clearly intended to talk to me, but I had never seen or noticed him before. I had my hands in my coat pockets to keep them warm, because I hate wearing gloves. When the man came closer he looked straight into my eyes and said "Hello."

"Hello," I replied. Not very original.

There was a pause as if he was remembering scripted lines.

"I am a taxi driver and I am always driving up and down this street," He said, pointing his finger towards the road to illustrate.

"Ah." What else was I supposed to say?

"I have been noticing you for months, you are always standing right here at exactly the same time. Always with your hands in your pockets," He said, smiling.

"Uh, okay," I said." I shifted my weight from left foot to right foot, something I tend to do when nervous.

"I am in love with you and I would like to ask you out for dinner," he stated in a matter-of-fact voice, as if he was asking the directions or commenting on the weather.

I looked to my right to examine that I was still inside the reality that I was in a few minutes earlier. Then I looked to my left and noticed that my bus was approaching. Then I got my gloveless right hand out of my pocket, pointed it at the bus and glanced briefly at the man in front of me and said, "Excuse me, I need to catch my bus."

I ran towards the number 24 bus as if my life depended on it. I was ready to push little old ladies out of my way and elbow the tall athletic young man ahead of me in order to be the first one to get on. As soon as I boarded, I began to shake. It wasn't what the man said that stunned me, it was the fact that he looked so much like Ismail. The smoothly combed black hair, the unusually pointy nose, the short legs and large torso, the muscular arms, the olive skin.

Taxi driver man looked more like Ismail than one of Ismail's own brothers looked like him. It was eerie. I wasn't planning to tell you about Ismail. It's a chapter of my life that I am trying earnestly to put in my rear-view mirror. But now this happens and all I can think about is him. I had done such a good job at forgetting about him for the last two weeks.

I met Ismail on a bus on my way home from work eight years ago. I was standing, he was sitting. He asked me to help him with his ESL homework. Since I was just standing there with nothing to do, I was happy to oblige. Anything to make a bus ride seem shorter is a treat. He had a conversation sheet which he dug out of his backpack and I helped him pronounce the sentences.

"Hello! My name is Ismail and I am from Morocco." He beamed a 50 kilowatt smile in my direction. How could I resist?

"Hello! Ismail, Nice to meet you. My name is Car." I could feel myself blushing with embarrassment at the stilted conversation.

"How do you do?" He was focusing so hard a knot formed between his brows.

"I am very well thank you." I wished I could kiss the spot right above his nose to get it unknotted.

"How are you?" Now he was repeating himself, but I didn't mind, not one bit.

"I am doing well," I replied, as if it was the most original question I had ever been asked.

I remember that stilted initial conversation like old reruns of the movie Casablanca. Ismail had a charming smile and a look in his eyes that drew me in the way a tide beckons the seagulls. Each time I corrected him he simply laughed at himself and tried to pronounce the words anew with a deliberation that made it sound more comical. By the end of the bus ride he asked if we could get together for a cup of coffee so that we could continue practicing his conversational skills. "Talking with native English speakers is important," he said, smiling at me, revealing white teeth like strung pearls. I timidly replied that I would be happy to help him. It was the smoothest pick up I ever witnessed. I gave him my phone number and one year later we were married. Ismail had few belongings. I don't think I ever imagined that anybody could survive with two pairs of jeans and four t-shirts as their main wardrobe. The only thing he had lots of was books. He moved in with a big pile of books in different languages. Since there wasn't enough space on my bookshelves, he piled all the books neatly on the bottom of his side of the closet. With so few other belongings, I couldn't complain about the books.

Then three months ago he moved out, taking his two pairs of jeans and his four t-shirts. He left behind the pile of books in my closet.

Now I am laying in my bed shivering. I will not call Ismail. I will not call Ismail. Car is strong. Be powerful. Vroom. Vroom. I don't own a phone. Phones have not been invented. Or maybe phones have been invented but declared sacrilegious. Now there is a

prohibition against phones. People who use phones risk jail. Sigin—
that is the word for prison in Arabic. Sigin sounds more musical
than the word prison. Using the phone at all tonight will send me
to sigin. Oh, I wish the phone would ring. I wish Ismail would call
me right now. Just to say "How are you doing?" or say anything. If
the phone rings I will pick it up. No, I will not pick up the phone.
Sigin is for answering the phone as well. Ismail call me. Call me.
Call me now.

That stupid taxi driver. I hope that his feet get dipped in
frozen ice and his hands in hot water and he is made to suffer the
torment of two extremes at once for what he did to me today. I hate
taxi drivers. They are all idiots. All that driving around day and
night sends them into a weird hazy world where streets and
buildings blend into one. All people mesh into a single continuous
nonsensical story. All that moving about while sitting in the same
spot on their asses. All those stupid tourists they must endure with
all their similar questions. Is there anything worse than a taxi driver?
Somebody who subverts the joy of driving a car into a pedestrian
way to earn a living. A taxi driver is worse than a prostitute. Do you
know what I hate about taxi drivers? They always want me to tell
them my life story. When I treat myself to a taxi ride, I want the
quiet that is missing from my daily bus ride. I am yet to meet a cab
driver who will grant me this simple pleasure. No sooner I am
settled in my seat salivating for a peaceful experience, the downpour
of questions begins: "Are you from out of town? Were you born
here? Where do you work? What do you do? Your name is Car?

That is a strange name. What nationality are you?" I do my best to answer each question politely but briefly—hinting at my desire for privacy. Please, please, please allow me the illusion that I am on my own in this car. One day I will meet a taxi driver who has zero interest in me. Who doesn't even want to know the story behind my name, because he doesn't know my name. I will hand him the address and he will just nod. When I arrive at my apartment building I'll pay him his fare and we will part in silence. We won't even exchange pleasantries. No "Goodbye, have a nice evening, thank you" ... none of that. That would be the dream cab ride. One day I will meet somebody capable of this, and I will take his phone number and contact him whenever I desire to treat myself. I will tip him double each ride. This nameless driver will become my favorite person on earth. Do such taxi drivers even exist? Perhaps I should search for a mute driver. I wonder what reaction I would get if I contacted Purple Cabs and asked them if they could send me a mute driver? Would that be considered rude?

It is useless. I can't sleep. I am going to go for a walk to turn this electric energy into exercise.

Scale Model

I GOT MESSAGES FROM both Steve and Yuri. Yuri even sent me a lacy lingerie and a vibrator. What makes him think I don't have one already? Whatever. Now I have two scheduled second dates: Steve on Friday night and Yuri on Saturday night.

I was day dreaming about my weekend dates on the bus, when the man sitting next to me rudely interrupted: "What are you smiling about?" He asked. I snapped back into my senses.

"Oh nothing, I was just remembering this video I saw online yesterday," I lied.

"Do tell," he insisted. Curious young man. Now I must remember something I saw.

"It was a video of a cow, an actual living cow, crossing a six-lane highway." Or was it a moose? I can't remember. There is bound

to be a video of both floating around the internet. So it doesn't matter.

The man looked concerned.

"No, don't worry, the cow makes it after a few near misses." I must seem like a monster because I think a near cow death is funny. Come to think of it, it's not funny at all. I should've come up with something less ghastly. But now it's too late.

"That reminds me of the video of an ostrich in France that tried to eat the side mirror of a car belonging to Russian tourists," he said. I hate that the video he remembers is more genteel. I wish he chose something ghoulish so that I wouldn't feel bad. But I pretend that I am amused by his story.

After a laughter punctuated conversation, the man introduced himself to me as Elliott. I in turn told him my name.

"Car. That's an odd name. What origin is that? Is that short for something?" Here comes the downpour of questions.

I get asked these questions with inquisitive looks that conceal cynical intentions. I answer them all dismissively: "It just is, that's my name." Nobody knows the story behind my name, except for Ismail. Nobody. Not even my mother. Now that Ismail is gone, I will tell you. Promise me you will not post this on facebook or blog about it. This is between me and you. Nobody needs to know it. Ok? For your ears only. It is not such a big deal. It's just private.

I was born Carmen Maria Franca. I was expelled from the womb of a Portuguese immigrant who landed in this country armed with a Portuguese husband. Mother left behind orange groves and the scent of freshly ground coffee to partake in the age of

modernity. She quickly slipped into the rhythms of motherhood and wife making that were different from her female lineage by the odd off-beat but maintained old fashioned phrasing.

My mother named me after an opera by some French dude who misunderstood Spanish culture. Advice to all mothers: "Don't name your children after a cultural artifact whose language you don't understand. It is a certain path to a disaster." I was named after a misunderstood cultural artifact of a misunderstood culture in a jambalaya of confusion. I was marked to be misunderstood the day that cursed name was bestowed on my birth certificate. Or maybe I was destined to misunderstand. Destined to appropriate somebody else's language and culture, mangle it out of shape to use it to suit sketchy purposes.

"Listen, listen to this!" my mother would whisper in hushed, urgent tones. "This is the part when they are in the tobacco factory." She would enunciate each syllable of the word *tobacco* as if Jesus himself was a tobacco factory worker. As if rolling cigarettes all day long was as glamorous as accepting an Oscar. I was ten before I finally had the wits to ask: "What are they saying?" I had assumed they were singing in Portuguese. "I don't really know," mother admitted, matter-of-factly. As if it is perfectly natural to not understand what you are listening to day in and day out. As if it is just fine to name your child after a tragedy whose depths you can't grasp. "It's in French," she'd say. It was a whole year later before I had the presence of mind to ask her why she enjoyed it so much even though she didn't understand a word. "You don't need to understand, you need to feel," she said, placing her hand over her

heart, like a defining moment in a Hollywood movie. It was the "You had me at Hello!" moment of my life. It was the "E.T. Go Home. Ouch!" moment of my childhood. "You don't need to understand, you need to feel," I told myself whenever I was befuddled. "I can feel this and that is enough." How stupid I was as a child.

I was 13 when I began to menstruate. Blood coming out an orifice I barely knew I had. What a cosmic joke! Can you think of a more bewildering way to signal the approaching train of adulthood? Who needs light at the end of a tunnel, when you can have blood at the end of your vagina?

My mother gave me a hug when I showed her my bloody panties. "Congratulations! you are now a woman," she said, warm as a duck feather duvet. One day later she came into my room wearing a gigantic smile and bearing two tickets. To celebrate my womanhood, the two of us—no boys allowed— were going to see a performance of Carmen at the Grand Opera House. My brother Albert didn't mind being excluded from this special occasion, not one bit, which should have been my first clue that it wasn't worth the fuss.

It was Friday night and I wore my best dress, a greyish blue chiffon number that wasn't suitable for the freezing cold winter night. I wore my everyday knee-length black coat. Back then same as now, I hated wearing gloves, so instead I placed my hands in my coat pockets and stepped out into the dark night to face the music with my mother.

I know that I am telling you this story with a cynical tone. I get that my mother meant well. I want to assure you that I am a rational and positive person. This part of my narrative is an aberration to the rest of me. So please do me the favor of reserving judgement.

I was squirming in my seat because of the menstrual cramps. My back muscles were experiencing one spasm after the other. My abdomen felt as if a hole was boring itself in my midsection. Plus, I still had blood coming out of my vagina. I was worried that I would leak into my seat through the sanitary pad and kept sticking my left hand beneath my bum to check for moisture. The grandeur of the place intimidated me. All the people attending the opera seemed far more important than myself. I felt small in my seat. I was a greyish blue chiffoned lady bug sitting on a big cushion, leaking red liquid from my bum. I wanted the performance to start so that I could forget my awkwardness. I anticipated an experience that would reveal my destiny. I was certain that my mother didn't name me after just any opera, but one that was sublime, one that would boost me into another plane of existence altogether. I hoped that I would be seeing secrets about my psyche. I was hungry for a revelation so crisp as to make all National Geographic photos seem like fussy hacks of an amateur at work. I wanted to be swept away. "This is big," I said to myself as the lights dimmed.

I took a deep breath.

The music seemed familiar. After all I had overheard it spewing out of the kitchen all my life. The visuals, however, were unlike anything I had imagined. Carmen was a scantly clad

seductress who riveted the attention of all the men on stage. She was wearing a corset and a peasant skirt that puffed up like a parachute swallowing air as she pranced about. Her body language didn't match the grand singing voice flowing out of her mouth. She was wild, savage, even vulgar. At one point she sat on a bench with her skirt twisted around her thighs and her legs parted. As she catches a man taking a peek up her hootchi kootchi, she laughs it off as if it's something that she enjoys. Did my mother name me after a tart? This is not what I was feeling when I heard the music wafting out of our kitchen along with the bacalhau à minhota and Cozido à portuguesa. Shock vibrated within every achy muscle in my body, making the pain more acute. I was hurting. Bleeding. Carmen was shouting about love.

Spoiler Alert

In the opera, Carmen gets killed. She is murdered by the man who claims to love her. In this production they made the death scene as realistic as possible. Fake blood was spewing out of her side. She was clutching herself. Shouting like a chicken that had lost its head. She looked like a car leaking engine oil. An old man on the left two rows down coughed. Her lover thrusted forward again, blood on his hands. Blood on Carmen's parachute skirt. Blood coming out of my vagina. It was all a big bloody mess. I suddenly felt an acute feeling in my crotch, as if a dam was holding back a gush. I imagined blood springing forth between my legs to drown Carmen, her lover, and all the musicians. Everybody in the opera swimming in my blood! What a disaster! Everybody screaming in distress. Shut the flow! Hold it in! The only people quiet are the

two Carmens. Me because I am happy I don't have to listen to the dreadful music anymore. Her because she is not being killed further. Or maybe because she is dead already. I can't decide. Either way she had a serene expression on her face. My blood is washing away her blood. The only happy people in the room are the Carmens. Let all the non-Carmens in the grand hall suffer. I don't care. Serves them right for wanting to watch this carnage. The musicians, the conductor, all the other singers, the back stage technicians, and most of all my mother. They all deserve to be swimming in the moist mucousy lining of my pre-pubescent womb.

I told my mother that I loved the opera and that it was the greatest experience of my life. I had no choice but assure her of her parental correctness. She was beaming as we rode the bus home. I resolved to change my name as soon as I was old enough to do so. At age 16, I declared that I wanted to be called Car to family and friends. I would register my annoyance whenever anyone forgot. My mom ignored my request for two weeks. After a hysterical shouting match, she acquiesced. I moved out of my mother's apartment right after high school so that I would never have to listen to that wretched music ever again. My apartment is a French composer-free zone. Opera. I hate opera. Refuse to listen to it. Go out of my way to avoid coming into contact with it. I even hate watching Oprah Winfrey on TV because her name reminds me of opera. My lone night at the opera was not a total waste. It taught me an important lesson. Feelings on their own are not enough. Devious creatures they are, these things called feelings. They can lead you astray. Waste your time with a bunch of non-sense. It was on that night

that I decided to become a rational person. Never again would I be betrayed by feelings. Science and logic are my bread and butter. I can solve any problem that faces me if I apply enough common sense to it. I don't want to feel it, I need to understand it.

And so when Ismail left I decided I would go about healing the broken heart in the most pragmatic way possible. There is a giant hole in my heart. I am depressed, and I know I am depressed. Something that I counted on so much and for several years invested the greater percentage of my energies to make it work has failed. There is no way to escape the feels. Now I know what you are thinking: "Oh no! Here comes the story of how a happy young woman turns into a sad lady with 25 cats." But I assure you there will be no cats in this story. Not a single one. I sat down at my desk and came up with a "how to heal a broken heart" plan. Like a business plan, my undertaking has spreadsheets, diagrams and a five-point contingency road map. I am taking this seriously. Yo!

Yield Sign

"... Yeah like I'm gonna..... I think I'm gonna like just send it again. Cos that guy, I think he, maybe he just didn't see it or it didn't get to him or something, he didn't just ignore it cos he's not the type to just ignore something like that. Yeah. Yeah. Heather Marie had a baby she named Olive, did you know that? Yeah! No, that was different, that was just someone I met on the street. Olive, yes. Some of us didn't know if it was a boy or a girl but 'I think it's a girl. ..."

God bless people who talk on their cell phones on the bus broadcasting their most private selves to a bunch of strangers. Honestly, I don't mind. Not as much as others do. The only part I find frustrating is the fact that I only hear one side of the conversation and have to guess the rest. I do realize it's none of my

business but in the above conversation I can't help myself. I want to know—is Olive a boy or a girl? What is the relationship between the young man speaking and Heather Marie? Why is he talking about her? What is he sending? My mind spins around like an engine. "I want answers!" I wish I could scream. "Don't just leave me hanging like this!"

My life bears a strange parallel to my sad state listening to this unintelligible half conversation. Ismail and I were married for 7 years. One day I came home to find a cryptic note on our dining table and him gone. I thought our marriage was fine. In fact I thought we were happy. Shock, disbelief, anger and hurt have all come and gone. Now the only thing I have left is confusion. Why? Why? Why? Why? Why did he leave? I don't understand. I tried to put it behind me, but it won't leave me alone. I need to answer the question before I move forward. I won't have any rest until I have an answer. I have long elaborate conversations with Ismail in my head. I remember things he said, things he did and then I construct this whole dialog in my imagination of us sitting together talking about our devastating split.

Another day to be thankful for cell phones on buses. Sounds like a horror movie—instead of *Snakes On A Plane*, it's *Cell Phones On A Bus*. A middle-aged woman sitting next to me leans over and says: "I heard about a commuter who carries on fake cell phone conversations in response to phone conversations going on around him." Perhaps that would've been amusing here, but it would've been hard to insert responses into the stream.

"You would have to be quick on your feet to do that," I whispered back to her. We both smile at each other now that we share a secret. "I wish I could see that in action. That would be a treat." I love that guy. Instead of feeling annoyed at not knowing half the story, the fake cell phone conversation commuter makes up his own story, entertaining everyone around him. I need to learn a lesson from his example.

Just so that you don't think I am all negativity, let's talk about something positive.

I love my boss. I sometimes think that I am the only person in the universe that likes her boss. Whenever I hear my friends complaining about work I feel guilty because I don't have a "my boss is such an idiot" story to share. Stephanie is awesome. I sometimes wish she wasn't my boss because then she would be my best friend. She is smart, straightforward and caring. Working as a technical writer in a software development company is harder than you might think. I have to write detailed descriptions explaining how software works. Most of the time I don't fully understand what I am attempting to explain. I have to depend on the computer programmers to explain it to me. Those geeks are always too busy working against a deadline and they never have time for the lowly documenter bothering them with stupid questions. "Nobody reads

the user documentation!" they say, dismissing me. "Just make something up, by the time we ship the docs the software will change again." If it wasn't for Stephanie it would be an uphill battle to stay motivated in this line of work.

"Everybody reads the user documentation," Stephanie insists. "They just deny it because they want to believe the users are smart enough to figure it out with a few clicks. Even programmers read the manuals because they can't remember what they programmed a few months earlier. They need reminders to help them figure out what the software is supposed to do."

"We are storytellers," Stephanie is fond of saying during staff meetings. "We take clicks and scrolls and translate them into real life scenarios that help people in their daily job routines. Without the story there would be only clicks and scrolls and it would all be meaningless."

I also work with Sam, whose real name is Samantha, but ever since she met me she decided to call herself Sam because she thinks it makes her seem cool. Sam is a super thin woman in her late twenties with stringy black hair flowing down her back. And then there is Cheryl who I'm guessing is in her forties. She is the minivan of women; plump and matronly. She has perfected the art of appearing to be working hard while doing the minimum possible to get by. The four of us are the documentors in this big labyrinth of cubicles. We are the lone women on this floor, tucked in the middle of a sea of geeks. Wave after wave of computer programmers to my left and even more computer programmers to my right. Anywhere I could throw a paper ball it might land on a geek. They say that these

guys are smart yet eccentric, and they (whomever they are) told the truth. I don't mind—neither the fact that they all think they are smarter than me, nor the fact that they are socially inept. In some strange way I find comfort in working with the likes of James, Ron, Ryan and Chris. I have learned to appreciate their Lord of the Rings obsession, show faint interest in their Star Wars posters and even laugh at their computer geek jokes. Thank goodness this is the age of Google. No need to ask "What does that mean?" each time one of them says something I don't understand. I note it down, nod my head as if Lady Galadriel was my second cousin and proceed knowing full well that my best buddy Google will turn all mystery into bite size knowledge ready for easy consumption.

Today Cheryl came to work late. I could hear her clothes rustling and her plastic bags making a squishy sound as they rubbed against each other. She is always carrying several plastic bags. I don't know why. She was huffing and puffing as she sat on her chair muttering to herself. "What a nightmare," she said, to nobody in particular. "Accident on the 96th. The police blocked the roads going both ways. It was a parking lot. Zen meditation, deep breathing, nothing helped. Nothing can prepare you for the self loathing you feel when stuck in traffic. No way to get out. I hate it! It makes me hate myself, hate humanity, hate civilization. Hate everything. I need to drink three lattes just to calm down."

Stephanie popped her head over the grey cubicle divider to my right and said, "Good morning gorgeous ladies! Team meeting in 15 minutes in the Oak room. Before you head to the lunch room to get

your morning coffees I need to warn you, the milk thief struck again."

Cheryl, Sam and I groaned. "Not again!" Sam said. "This is the worst day ever," said Cheryl.

Some annoying person in our office steals all the milk from lunch room, which means that everybody has to adjust to either drinking coffee without milk or buying coffee from the nearby coffee shop until Jennifer the office manager can get out to buy more. Either way, it's annoying. Why would somebody steal eight cartons of milk every couple of weeks? What is he doing with it anyway? Bathing in it?

At the meeting, with milk-less coffee, we all took our habitual places at the table. I sit with my back to the wall, at the middle of the table. Cheryl sits next to the door, ready to pop up should the phone ring, part of the illusion she tries to create that she's actually working. Sam, the last in, sits by me.

"We have been handed a new project," said Stephanie.

"Great! More work for me," said Cheryl. As if!

"You will be glad to know that I decided to assign Excalibur to Car," Stephanie said, smiling. Cheryl wheeled herself to face the rest of us instead of the corridor and leaned her elbows on the table. Samantha looked at me with her mouth open. I took a deep breath and then said: "Great! When do I begin?"

Excalibur is the remote sensing project headed by Chris. Stephanie asked me to meet with him, read the all existing documentation and start putting an outline for the user

documentation together. I see this as a vote of confidence. Starting documentation from scratch is hard work. In the past it was always Cheryl that started new documentation. Clearly she thinks that I am up for the task. I walked away from our meeting filled with eager energy. I skipped all the way to Chris's office to get started.

Engine

I HAD A FANTASTIC WEEKEND, yet here I am riding the bus to work on a Monday morning feeling morose. I don't know what is wrong with me. My date with Steve was lovely. He made a reservation at a steak house. Not very fancy, but I prefer it that way. He was sweet and gentlemanly. He got out of his seat when I walked in the restaurant and even adjusted my chair for me to sit comfortably. He talked about his ex, even referring to her as his wife a few times. But I don't mind. By our age, everybody has an ex they are trying to forget about. I am no different. I just have the good sense to keep it to myself. I am proud to report that I didn't mention Ismail, not even once. Steve told me that his ex was his true soul mate. Despite the intense connection they had, she decided she needed to separate from him because he was weighing

her down. She wanted to explore a little before she settled down again. It was she who instructed him to go out on a few dates. "Make yourself less boring," were her marching orders, he said. He seemed to think that once both of them experimented around they would get back together. Something about this strikes me as romantic. Devotion to the wife that walked away.

My date with Yuri ended up with sex, as expected. We ate dinner at an Italian place. Then he drove me to his place and offered me a drink. The moment I stepped into his apartment we were both on top of each other. The sex was ok, but not great. You might think given his level of hotness he would be absolutely amazing in bed, but there is no need to judge a man based on first experience. The next morning, he made me breakfast and we agreed we would see each other again, but we didn't set a firm date.

"You smell so bad!" A young man at the front of the bus yelled at the woman sitting opposite him. "Why didn't you take a shower this morning?" The young woman widened her eyes and opened her mouth. She just stared at him and blinked. Blinked and stared. At one point she made a sound as if she was about to say something, all she managed to utter was "ah..." and then she inhaled deeply and shut her mouth again. Another young woman standing next to her jumped in when it became apparent that the object of his derision

was unable to defend herself. "Hey, no judgement!" She said. "You don't know what kind of a day she's had so far. You have no right to put her on the spot like that." An elderly man followed that up with "That's right!" The most amazing thing happened next. Nothing. The odious, odor-obsessed man crossed his arms in front of his chest looked down at his feet and did absolutely nothing. I was certain that he was itching for a fight. He looked like the edgy type searching for a release. Yet when presented with the opportunity on a silver platter he stepped back. Goes to prove that you never know about human nature. You think you have a map that guides you through the city. But when you discover yourself in a place you don't want to be, you realize you had the wrong map all along. You can never guess what somebody will do in a difficult situation. Which reminds me of Antar.

It was Ismail who told me the story of Antar one evening during the first year of our marriage. I was tossing and turning in bed, unable to sleep. Ismail turned on the bed-side lamp and looked at me inquisitively yet kindly: "What's wrong with you tonight? It's after midnight."

"I can't sleep, my mind is wired," I said, wearily.

"Let me see if I can unwire it for you," he said. There was a pause. I wondered what he was planning to do. He gestured that I should lay my head on his shoulder. Then he stroked my side affectionately. Calm wrapped round and round my body like a bunch of bumper cars. He began to tell me a story in his gentle whirring voice—*The story of Antar*

Where I grew up everything that happened before the advent of Islam is called Asr Al Jahiliya (age of ignorance). And thus, it's dismissed as unworthy of knowing. The pharaohs, the Babylonians and a whole slew of civilizations—they're just wiped under the carpet and ignored. It's hard for some to reconcile the idea that in the Middle East, there were great societies, wellsprings of knowledge and even refined manners, before Islam. Sure, the ancient civilization of Sumer invented writing. And yeah, the ancient Egyptians invented graffiti. But how refined could those people really be? How valuable was their knowledge? When their minds had not yet been illuminated, by insightful eloquence of a single verse of the Quran?

However, there are some stories so compelling that a mountain of religious pride can't prevent the waves of retelling to seep through from one generation to the next. This story, the story of Antar, which I am about to tell you is one such story.

In fact, I have read in a history book in a dusty old library back home that when the prophet Mohammed heard the story of Antar, he was so impressed by the nobility of his spirit, he declared in awe, "I have never yearned more to meet a man in person."

Prepare yourself, my dear wife, you are about to hear a story like no other: Historically correct, yet of such mythical proportions that had Shakespeare, Scheherazade and Steven Spielberg knocked their heads together for one thousand and one nights they could not have produced a more satisfying narrative. For a mountain moved to meet prophet Mohammed, but do you think the chosen one was moved by just any tale?

Antar, whose full name is Antarah Ibn Shaddad al Absi was born in the 6th century in Najd—the northern part of what is now Saudi Arabia. His mother Zabibah was a black slave from Africa and his father was ..... well! ... back then people didn't ask the son of a slave who his father was. It was a rude question or at least an inconvenient one. For only free men got to boast of heritage and lineage and a slave was just a slave. A child born into slavery only knew for certain who his mother was. When Antar was born he was called Antar son of Zabibah, but most members of the tribe of Bani Abs didn't bother remembering his name. He was called *Hey You!*, *Boy*. He was summoned with shouts and finger snaps.

There was something exceptional about Antar right from the start. At first only his mother noticed. But quickly it became hard to disguise. By age nine he could pick up a stray sheep and carry it on his shoulders back to the flock. By age twelve he could carry four pails of water all at once without a rest, while grownup slaves carried them one by one. After that, he just grew and grew and grew. He became tall and strong. His muscles pulsated with the yeasty energy of rising bread. His curly hair shined in the sun. He was full of raw brutish physicality. Then one day everything changed by an unexpected encounter. Antar was refilling the water jug in his master's tent. In the sleeping quarters he caught a glimpse of his master's wife combing the hair of a young woman called Abla. Abla's hair was smooth as silk and flowed like a reed mat. Her restrained giggles reminded Antar of the song of the nightingale. Her skin was the color of wheat. Her eyes were more alluring than the eyes of a gazelle. She had many folds, bumps and curves in her body. A

sudden feeling of weakness came over Antar. His muscles felt like dough. His blood began to flow like spoiled milk. That night Antar went to bed in feverish daze and when he woke up the next morning, the strangest thing came out of his mouth. It was poetry.

Before I continue this story, I need to explain something. You know the old proverb "If the prophet Mohamed won't go the mountain, the mountain must come to Mohamed"? Well that proverb is unfamiliar to us from the Middle East because it was made up in the West. When God decided to impress the Arabs he couldn't use the usual tricks he used in the past to impress other people. Healing the sick, raising the dead or parting a sea—That was just a magic show for kids. The Almighty knew that these were hardened desert people who saw sand dunes move in front of their eyes and where a few drops of water created the greatest miracle of all—life. Do you think these people would have been impressed with a moving mountain? Naaaah! When God needed to get the attention of the Arabs, he knew he had to work harder. Become extra creative. He would have to impress with a perpetual miracle that would dazzle them for thousands of years to come. These hardened desert folks forget quickly. And so God inspired the words of magnificent eloquence that are the Quran. The only miraculous ability bestowed on this prophet was the ability to open his mouth and utter words arranged in a perfect geometry of beauty and meaning. I am telling you this because I am trying to impress on you the importance of poetry in Arabic culture. In this cultural context, over time, Antar would become one of the top poets of Arabia. Before Islam, there were seven poems that were displayed in the

kaaba (the most secret shrine in Islam today). These poems, back then, were considered the finest examples of Arabic poetry. Antar would attain the distinguished honor of being one the poets in this exclusive club.

I am skipping ahead. Let's go back to Antar's dazed confusion. Encountering Abla awakened in Antar not only poetry, but a sense of nobility. Antar became the first practitioner of the power of positive thinking. Perhaps he is the one who invented it. Long before the book *The Secret* was published, Antar decided that he would visualize everything that his heart desired and then proceed to behave as if his dreams were realities on the ground. As such, from that day on, Antar behaved as if he was a high nobleman of Bani Abs and he expected people to treat him accordingly.

People who loved Antar tried to dissuade him from his foolish ways. Zabibah, his brother Shieboob and other slave friends told him: "Be reasonable. Get your head out of the clouds." Antar didn't listen.

He stormed into his master's tent and asked him: "Hey Shadad! Are you not my father?" Shadad gasped with horror and beat him within inches of his life. From then on, Antar referred to him as "father" and Shadad would beat him each time, until he got tired of the whole exercise and simply ignored the offensive word that his slave was in the habit of using.

One day Antar went to the sword maker and asked him for a sword. The sword maker laughed. "What need does a slave have with a sword when all he does is herd sheep and carry water?" He explained to Antar what was obvious: "Swords are for warriors. A

free man has something to fight for because he has something to lose. What does a slave have to lose? Nothing. If we are raided by another tribe you will simply be the slave of another master." Antar punched him and ransacked his workshop. The sword maker finally relented and made a wooden training sword for Antar: "Here is your toy sword for your pretend warrior games."

Antar would steal away during free time behind a giant rock in the outer edges of his tribe's encampment and there he would practice swinging his pretend sword around. Swishing it in the wind. Slicing the air. Attacking sand dunes. Fantasizing about becoming one of the great warriors of his time.

One day the tribe Hat raided Bani Abs. All the brave warriors saddled up their horses and rode off to fight the enemy. Antar was left behind as usual. Some of the women took advantage of the absence of husbands, fathers and brothers and decided to go to the oasis to have a little party. The women dismissed any danger with giggles: "We have full trust in courage of our men, they are the bravest in all Arabia." The women's-only merriment was proceeding joyfully, when 20 of the Hat warriors arrived intending to capture the women for slaves. "Help! Help!" Abla called out. When Antar heard her voice a volcanic rage overcame him. He grabbed the man that was attempting to kidnap Abla by the neck and proceeded to strangle him with his bare hands. He took his attacker's sword and fought single handily against the rest of the 20 men. As he hacked and sliced with clothing soaked in blood, Antar roared like a lion. Those who didn't run away in defeat were killed.

When all was over, all the Bani Abs women took turns thanking Antar for rescuing them, calling him a hero. Each one looked at him with new admiration. Finally, it was Abla's turn to acknowledge him. Her hips swayed from side to side as she walked towards him. She looked at him with those mesmerizing eyes and touched his forearm with her finger. Antar took a deep breath, for his torment was unbearable. He had defeated 20 men and roared like a lion. Abla's touch turned him into melted butter. His feet could barely support him. "Thank you Antar," she said in her honeyed voice that conveyed meanings within meanings. "I will make sure that everybody in the tribe knows of your courage today." Antar was lucky he didn't faint as she sauntered away towards her tent.

When the leader of the tribe, Sheik Malik, heard of what happed at the oasis he immediately ordered Antar to appear before him. Feeling honored, Antar kneeled before the sheik. The Sheik fed Antar rice with lamb meat cooked in milk with his own hand—a gesture of respect. The Sheik would roll up a bite size portion of meat mixed with the meat stew and plop it into Antar's mouth as thanks for saving the tribe's women and with it the tribe's honor. On that day Antar became a free man. He was awarded a horse called Abjar. A special sword was commissioned for him called Al Thamie, which means The Thirsty One. Antar was happy but not satisfied. There was one more thing he desired on that day the sheik couldn't give him. He approached Shadad and asked to be acknowledged as his son. After hesitation, Shadad conceded. "I hope you will do a better job obeying me as my son than you did as my

slave," he said, biting his lips and shaking his head with disbelief at his own words.

From then on Antar son of Zabibah became Antar Ibn Shadad. But all was not well among the tribe of Bani Abs. A more difficult challenge lay ahead.

Try to put yourself in the shoes of any of the young men of Bani Abs. Each trying to prove himself to his father and his community. Each one dreaming of becoming a sung hero earning looks of admiration from young women. And then, out of nowhere, marches in a slave of little preparation and much disadvantage grabbing all the limelight. There was much resentment brewing in the tents of Bani Abs that night and many nights to follow. Everywhere Antar went whispers trailed behind his back: "He is not one of us, look at him, he is black."

Antar was busy with a different matter altogether. Behind the giant rock where he practiced his sword he was now practicing a set of new moves. Daily he met Abla regaling her with his poetry, stealing kisses and playing entertaining games. Laughter entered Antar's heart. Life became the pouring rain that the deserts crave.

Assured of Abla's feelings towards him, Atar gathered all his courage and proceeded to ask for his beloved's hand in marriage from her father. Abla's father wasn't enthusiastic about the prospects. But instead of simply refusing, he devised a clever plan. One that would get rid of the wretched man that had enchanted his daughter once and for all. He said yes. As a dowry for his daughter, he asked for three thousand red camels. Red camels are rare and the only person who ever owned such a beautiful herd was king Noaman

of Iraq. Abla's father thought: "If Antar doesn't die crossing the desert, he will certainly be killed by the mighty king while attempting to steal his herd." This was truly mission impossible.

Antar charged forward with the aid of his trusty horse through sand storms, across sand dunes, nearly perishing in a quicksand pit. Upon emerging barely alive in Iraq he was taken hostage while attempting to steal the camels. Soldiers placed Antar in front of king Noaman in chains.

"Who dares steal from me?" The king asked in anger. Antar identified himself. The king was stunned. "You are Antar? The man whose reputation has crossed the desert? The Antar I heard of is brave and honorable. The Antar I heard of is not a thief."

Antar was struck by raging emotions at this accusation. It hurt to be called a thief. It hurt that his whole entire life he was treated like garbage simply because his skin was black. It hurt that time and again he rescued his people in battle yet they continued to deride him as an inferior. He wasn't stupid! He knew full well that Abla's father was attempting to get rid of him. Antar remembered all the beatings he had received as a slave. All the indignity he had endured. He had worked so hard to earn his freedom. Yet here he was again, in chains, humiliated, all because his people were unable to accept him as one of their own. It would have been easy for him to feel angry, bitter even. It would be natural to seek revenge. It would have been easy for him to hate all of Bani Abs. But there was this love, this yearning in his heart for Abla. No matter how much he despised his treatment at the hands of the Bani Abs, he was unable to feel anything but love towards the tribe that formed the family of

his beloved. All that emotion twisted and knotted in his chest. Inside his belly there was a simmering ready to boil over. In that moment, it burst forth in words of poetry. Antar gave himself to it.

ولجَّ اليومَ قومُكِ في عذابي   ألا ياعبلُ قد زادَ التصابيْ

كما ينْمو مشيبي في شَبابي   وظلَّ هواكِ ينمو كلَّ يومٍ

King Noaman heard these words and was transported to a time when he too was a young man and stupid in love. He heard the anguish in Antar's voice. The poetry conveyed the depths of the injustice that he suffered. This is the point in the story where we get discover what was truly exceptional about Antar. It wasn't his unprecedented physical strength. It wasn't his bravery in battle. It wasn't the eternal eloquence. It wasn't even the inspiring romance. What was truly exceptional about Antar was the nobility of his spirit. Whenever presented with a tough choice he allowed himself to be driven by love instead of hate.

The king begged Antar to stop, afraid he would start crying, and offered him a deal: "I will give you the three thousand red camels. In return, you will fight in my army for two years." Antar agreed heartily. This was the first time Antar had been offered a fair deal. So this is how, three years after leaving his home, he returned with camels, servants, silks, treasure, perfume, jewellery and riches the likes of which nobody in Bani Abs had ever seen before.

Finally Abla's father had no choice but to relent. All the noble men of Arabia were now afraid to ask for Abla's hand in fear of Antar's wrath. Antar's rejoicing was short-lived, however, as Abla stated that she had her own requirement before marriage. "What?"

Antar said, bewildered. "I have brought you three thousand red camels, riches, treasures, and servants. What more could you possibly want?" Abla waved her hand dismissively. "That is nothing. You did all those things to impress my father. Now you have to do something to impress me."

Abla continued explaining her demand:

"Among the women of Arabia there is a raging debate going on. Those with sense say that I am the most beautiful woman in the desert. Those that lack it claim that Jaida bint Zahir of Bani Zubaid is even more beautiful. I want you to go capture Jaida so that she can become my servant on my wedding night. Everybody coming into my tent to congratulate me on my nuptials will be able to see us side by side. That will dispel whatever doubt there is about my rightful title as the queen of the Sahara."

"Was there ever a woman harder to impress?" Thought Antar.

Poor Antar did as was asked of him.

They had a lavish wedding that lasted for ten days and nights and was attended by dignitaries from far and wide. I could happily state "The End" at this point and let you fantasize about a happily ever after. But alas, your storyteller reads too many books and researches his stories thoroughly. Any time two strong willed people are united by the bonds of marriage, sparks fly. Antar and Abla had a passionate relationship but also fought like cats and dogs. When things got heated between them Abla would ridicule him, saying "When I met you, you were a nothing but a slave. I am the daughter of a nobleman." Antar had a few choice words as ammunition as well. Abla was unable to conceive children. Antar wasn't shy to

remind her that she was a failure as a woman. Despite her beauty and nobility she lacked the most important thing that a woman should possess. Eventually Antar married a second wife to satisfy his desire for offspring.

In case you are worried about Jaida bint Zahir, things turned out alright for her. Proving to be a complete failure as a servant, Antar returned her to her husband a few days after the wedding.

Antar died in battle close to his 90th birthday. He died same way as he lived—exceeding his contemporaries in all that they held dear: Nobility, eloquence, courage and romance, but all the same never quite accepted by his own people."

Ismail ended the story by instructing me to close my eyes. He covered me with blanket and whispered: "Sweet dreams, dear wife."

I frequently reflect on the story of Antar. Right now I feel like Antar in chains kneeling before King Noaman. Rejected and abandoned. We all know what would Antar do if he was in my place? He would take his sword and fight his adversary. Write poetry to win his beloved's heart. Sadly I am not good at either of these things.

But then I wonder if when Ismail told me this story he didn't identify with Antar. Perhaps this story captured his sense of feeling discriminated against, living in this society. Perhaps I didn't

understand how painful it was for him. My heartbreak healing plan includes remembering all the bed time stories that Ismail told me during our marriage. Perhaps If I remember all of them I will be able to decipher why he left. Perhaps that will help me move forward with my life.

My encounter with Chris about the Excalibur project was strange. I found him hunched over his keyboard clutching a stress toy in his left hand and forcefully hitting the delete button while muttering: "Bitch, bitch, all wrong bitch," presumably directed to his computer.

"Hey Chris!" I said, straining not to jump up and down with excitement. "How are you doing?"

"Hey, Car! To what do I owe the pleasure of this visit?" Chris said, straightening up.

"I have just been assigned the Exalibur project," I said. "I will be your documenter."

"Congratulations!" He said. "But are you worthy of the honor of documenting Excalibur?"

I laughed, in on the joke. "Well probably not, but I am the one working on it. "I told him what I'd need to get started."

"Not good enough. You have to prove your worth before I hand over the project," Chris said with a crooked smile on his face. I guess he was enjoying himself.

"How do I do that?"

"Arthur had to pull the sword from a stone to prove he was the rightful king. You, young lady, you must prove your value to

inherit the project." Chris went back to hunching over his keyboard, ignoring me.

After about twenty seconds, I realized that he was serious. But he hadn't specified what I had to do to receive his cooperation. I walked back to my desk feeling like a tire whose air had been let out.

Bus

THE BUS STOP SITS conveniently right in front of the doorway
to my apartment building. Did I choose the right apartment
building to live in, or what? All I need to do to catch the bus to
work in the morning, is step out of the front door and there it is.
My trusty 14 line is punctual. I take the 7:43 am straight to
downtown, arriving at my desk around 8:13 am. There is a class of
bus riders that I call "The Vulnerables". They are the mentally ill
who speak to invisible ghosts that those of us with feet firmly
planted in reality can't see, aimless drifters who ride the bus but
have no destination, fare dodgers who want to ride for free and
spout obscenities to high heaven when caught and asked to leave the
bus, those who smell bad and don't care about hygiene, those who
care about hygiene a little too much, with their sanitary wipes and

alcoholic hand gels. And those who get on a bus with vacant eyes and souls whose process of reclamation shall be long and hard. And then there are people like me, simply getting through the daily grind. In this soup of humanity, I dissolve every day at least twice. Each time I emerge a little changed by the encounter. I am a good listener, I have been told many times in the past. Everywhere I go, people want to sit next to me to tell me their life's story. The truth is I enjoy listening to other people's stories, even the annoying ones, even the old lady who wants to show me the cute pictures of her adorable cat. Strangely, I find it interesting.

Today I met Sylvester. He struggled getting up on the bus because of his cane. He grabbed both handles with both arms while letting his cane dangle by a strap on his right wrist. He heaved himself on the first step with a force that seemed unbecoming of his age. Then he hobbled over and sat right next to me. Sylvester was wearing a tweed jacket, tailored pants and a white cotton shirt. He smelled faintly of fine aftershave. His smile radiated in my direction and he introduced himself. I told him my name which he acknowledged with a soft nod. He told me he was a retired traffic engineer on his way to meet his other retired traffic engineer buddies for a coffee. The five of them meet every Tuesday. How cute! Old colleagues continuing with a friendship long after retirement. I wonder if there is somebody at my job I would want to see weekly after I left work. Stephanie maybe. But I suspect that Stephanie would be too busy with work, husband and her children. She wouldn't have time to meet with me that frequently. I admire

Sylvester for building such strong friendships through his work. I asked him what inspired him to become a traffic engineer.

"When I was a boy I thought sociology was the most interesting topic of study," he said. "It deals with the how individuals interact with society and how society shapes the individuals. You might be right to think that anthropology is a more interesting topic. Because with anthropology you study exotic cultures from faraway lands and all their unusual customs. However, there is nothing more exotic than learning about what is happening in your own backyard. You would be amazed at the historical origins of some of our customs. Why is it that we behave the way we do? Did you know, for example, that the way a city is planned will affect how the people living in it will relate to each other? Or how a person feels about himself? Look at the curve of the pavement at that intersection," he said, pointing a wrinkled finger out the window. "It's designed to be inviting to pedestrians. The elevation of pavement compared to the street level has been studied by experts to optimize appeal to pedestrian yet create safety by repelling cars without being too obtrusive. Once I realized how I can impact people's lives profoundly in this invisible manner, without them even realizing it, I just knew that was the job for me."

His eloquent, thoughtful answer surprised me. I expected him to talk about cars and love of driving them. It almost brought me to tears. I wish I had such a sense of purpose in what I do.

Sylvester suggested that I give him my mailing address so that he could send me a special gift to help me with my urban exploring.

I scribbled my address on a piece of paper and handed it to him. He folded it neatly and placed it in his pocket.

I like arriving early at the office because it gives me a few minutes in the morning where it's possible for me to imagine that the whole place belongs to me. I sit at my desk and savour the moments of quiet.

Today, I dedicated the morning to thinking about a scheme to convince Chris to hand over Excalibur. I Googled *How did king Arthur choose his knights?* My thinking being that Chris mentioned King Arthur, and if he is King Arthur, I should become one of his Knights. I was certain this would flatter his ego. After an hour of reading a bunch of stories online I concluded that I would have to save a damsel in distress to prove my worth. I don't immediately know anybody that requires saving, so what am I to do? I thought about dressing up like a knight with a plastic sword. It seemed like too much effort. What would Antar do? Antar would grab his sword and demand the documentation by force. Unfortunately, that is illegal and would probably get me fired.

I walked outside the office building to clear my thinking. My legs took me to the corner of Fairhaven road and Sunshine street where I stood to watch the traffic.

One car.

Two car.

Red car.

Blue car.

From Sudan to India,

Traffic flows all around.

This one has a broken wing.

This one looks like a shiny coin.

Some are bad.

Others are sad.

Why? you ask they are sad and bad.

I don't know. Go ask an expert.

Some have something to say about those who ride them.

This one says: "I compensate for a short shift stick."

This one says: "I have no kids."

You might see it as nothing but metal and gas.

But we have lives that rattle and smash.

We kiss and frolic.

In a round about way.

You call it a fender bender.

We love the sound of metal as it cracks.

Look!

Look!

There goes an eggplant purple hatchback.

It has green grass glued to the hood.

I believe the driver is as giddy as a ferris wheel.

You should see us when we dance.

We swerve, tango and then collapse.

You call it a disaster crash.

We don't mind.

O the fun we had.

There once was a green car called little pistachio.

Pistachio felt lonely.

It drove around and around.

And there was nobody to hang around.

But then a red car called wild horse appeared on the scene.

Horse was strong,

had shiny doors and unique tires.

Everything about it made eyes pop.

Little pistachio couldn't believe her luck

such a prime specimen would even notice her.

They clacked doors.

Waved their windshield wipers at each other

and pretty soon where inseparable.

They danced the waltz together.

Went to the movies.

That first kiss was electric.

Shorty after there were new cars.

Little ones.

Big ones.

Blue,

white

and yellow.

And together they were making beautiful traffic jams.

They would stand in perfectly aligned lines.

All the passengers screamed and shouted.

"The pollution is killing the environment."

They didn't care.

Because they had each other.

After 20 minutes of traffic contemplation I realized that I should do the sensible thing and ask Stephanie for advice. I stood at her door, which is always open, waiting for her to invite me in. She beckoned me in mid coffee sip. She tried to say "come in" while swallowing but only a mumbling sound came out. Ehmmmm mmmm mm in. Her clumsy mannerism is so charming it verges on being adorable. I sat down to tell her the whole story and told her that I felt unable to come up with an idea to prove my worth to Chris. Stephanie told me to leave it with her. "Don't respond. Don't do anything. I will make sure he is dealt with," she said, sounding personally offended with Chris for questioning her judgement. Isn't my boss great? I knew that talking it over with her was a good idea.

I went back to my desk, intending to write a message to Steve letting him know that I won't be seeing him again. I need to make room in my dating schedule for new candidates. I wrote the nicest rejection email I could.

"Dear Steve,

It was lovely meeting you for dinner the other day. You are kind, funny and an engaging conversationalist. However, I don't think that we are good match for each other. Another woman will be lucky to have you in her life.

Sincerely,

Car"

Ten minutes later I got his reply.

"I knew you were a whore the minute I saw you." Oh boy! Please don't beat around the bush and tell me what you really think.

Sending a rejection to a man is the hardest thing in the world. No matter how gently and sensitively I try to do it, it always ends with me being called a whore or some other unmentionable name. At least on-line, I can simply ignore the abusive emails. My options are these: I can ignore his stupid email and hope we both simply forget about it over time. Or I can send him back an email calling him a sexually frustrated douchebag who needs to get over his ex. But then I am a sexually frustrated douchebag who needs to get over her ex as well. So who am I to judge? My third option is to tell him that I changed my mind and want to see him again just to see if he would believe me. The amusing ideas I have.

I will ignore him.

Driving Lesson

DAVID IS MY DRIVING INSTRUCTOR. He is a middle-aged talkative cheerful fellow. He speaks in gentle even tones that never alarm. He has been teaching me how to drive for three years with a positivity that borders on the pathological. I am his greatest source of income and his greatest frustration. One day when I pass my driving test I will become his greatest achievement. I love my bi-weekly rides with David. It gives me the thrilling experience of driving a car. At this point he has covered all the safety basics with me at least five times and there isn't much to teach me. Each ride we end up chatting. He tells me a little about himself and I tell him a little about myself. In this way, much of our driving involves laughter. I drive, we talk and then we laugh and laugh and laugh. David has a great sense of humor. He should be a comedian. He

loves to make fun of himself or tell me jokes about other driving instructors. I will miss my driving lessons once I get my driving license because of all the levity that it brings to my life.

I wait for David outside my apartment building, next to the bus stop. He pulls up with a cheerful smile. "Hop in!" He says, jumping out of the car and moving to the passenger seat.

Oh the rush! Turning the engine on, feeling the buzz. It makes me feel tingly all over. I am actually driving a car. It is not my car. It is not pistachio green. But I am actually really driving a car. Not in my imagination. Not inside a video game. Not a fantasy. Real, 3D, physical world, tire on tar, driving. I love driving in heavy traffic. The long pauses followed by brief movement. The exhilarating feeling you get when you can finally drive for a long stretch. Do you know the song *Life is a Highway* by Johnny Cochrane? I love that song. I have listened to it a bazillion times. It has to be my favorite song in the world. Has there ever been poetry more evocative than this? "Life is a highway, I am gonna ride it all night long." I play that song in my imagination whenever I am with David. I think it's the reason our rides together are always so happy. Too bad that Ismail never wanted to make love to that song. We tried once. "It interrupts my rhythm," he had said. He wanted something slow and soulful, if anything at all. In fact, he preferred no musical accompaniment at all.

"Hey guess what?" David said. "I got a letter from my ex-wife, all the way from Indonesia. It had a picture of my son, he is eight now."

"That's great. He must be beautiful," I said with eyes firmly facing forwards. David frowns upon me looking at him while driving.

"Most beautiful boy in the world. I will show you the picture once we are parked safely." He tapped the dashboard with his index finger in a musical rhythm.

I slowed down for a yellow light.

"Do you know what the most amazing thing about your culture is?" David stopped tapping.

"What culture are you talking about?" The light turned red and I allowed myself a glance sideways at him.

"You know. Muslim culture," David said.

"Muslim is not a culture, it is a religion," I said, feeling smug at my political correctness.

"Yeah! whatever, you know what I mean." The light turned green. David pointed forward to draw my attention to it.

"I am not Muslim, by the way." I pressed on the gas pedal.

"But you were married to one, weren't you? Didn't he force you to convert?" David looked into the side mirror to check while I changed lanes.

"No, I never converted. Ismail is an atheist. I told you before." I turned off my right-hand signal.

"Maybe he didn't want to follow the rules, but I am sure that he wanted his wife to be religious and cover her head." He looked into the rear-view mirror to check that I was keeping pace with the traffic.

"No, no, no Ismail is nothing like that. He is a true atheist. Religion nauseated him. We had nothing to do with religion." I shook my head.

"Well anyway, in Muslim culture, as you know, the father gets custody of his son when he reaches the age of nine. All I have to do to get custody of my son is convert to Islam, go to Indonesia, and demand my son in court. My ex-wife wouldn't be able to do a thing to stop me." David strummed his index finger on his seatbelt.

"I didn't know that," I said, stopping for a pedestrian.

"So I asked some of them religious leaders like priests, only this guy wears a turban and has a bushy beard. I went to that place, what do you call it? temple ....like an Islam church?" David's eyes were on the young man crossing the road.

"Mosque." I gradually hit the gas pedal.

"Yes, so this bushy beard guy told me that I could convert to Islamic Culture if I say some mumbo jumbo and he would declare me Islamic. Can you believe it? It's that easy. Did your ex have a beard like that?" David scratched his chin.

"No, he was clean shaven." I shook my head.

"Strange, I thought all the men from your culture had beards. Isn't it a sign of manhood?" David now scratched the other cheek.

"You know, David, I am from here. I am from the same culture as you." I turned on the left-hand signal.

"Yes, but you married one of them." David placed both hands in his lap.

"So did you!" I waited for an opening to turn and took it.

"I never thought about it that way. We have this thing in common," said David.

Ok, so David is an ignorant fellow and sometimes he says things that deviate into that territory that smells of racism. But he is well meaning. He's a good guy. It isn't his fault he wasn't born with a high IQ. I really, really like him. He is fun to be around. There is just one thing that he does that bugs me. He constantly compares me to his ex-wife. I might say something like: "I love to eat sushi" and he will react: "That's strange, my ex refused to eat it." As if I am supposed to be a carbon copy of his ex-wife. As if all Muslim women are exactly the same, have the same opinions, tastes, moods and mannerisms. I am not even Muslim. I was married to an atheist who was raised by a Muslim family. I lived in Morocco for three short months. But I am not Muslim. I am not from Indonesia. And I am probably nothing like his ex.

Outside of talking about his ex who abandoned him abruptly and left with their son back to her country of origin, David loves to talk about popular music, movies and he tells wicked jokes. If David stopped comparing me to that other woman, we would become best friends.

I am so grateful for my driving lesson with David today because it counter balances the unpleasant day I had at work. Chris stomped over to my desk. I could feel the vibrations under my feet even before he showed up. His face was red. His nostrils flared, revealing a great hairy maze.

"You ungrateful opportunist," he spat. I was so stunned I didn't say anything.

"I was treating you like a member of my team, but you think you are above that." The anger stood between us like a concrete wall.

"What are you talking about?" I said, my voice as feeble as a made in China toy car at the dollar store.

"You had your boss talk to my boss to dress me down." I could see my reflection in his eyes looking down on me. That's a mirror I will avoid looking into in the future.

"No I didn't," I said. "I simply asked Stephanie for advice on how to prove my worthiness for the project."

"Well! You certainly have failed in the most pathetic way possible. You are not worthy of my beautiful invention. King Arthur would have chopped your head off and stuck it on a spike." He bent over as if he wanted to spit the words on top of my head.

"I can see that you are angry. But in my defence ..." He cut me off mid-sentence. Too bad I couldn't tell him what Antar would have done to him since he doesn't know who Antar is.

"Stop!" He said, like one of the Supremes. He raised his stop sign hand towards my face. He was looking down at me exactly like a diva. Diana Ross herself would have envied the theatrics.

"No defence is necessary. You shall get what you wanted. Everything I have will arrive in your email shortly. Good luck figuring it out without my help."

He did a little twirl to give me his back like a ballerina. It would have been graceful if he hadn't stomped off like a bulldozer.

Sam popped her head over the cubicle divider. "What was that about?" Cheryl walked over and sat at my desk. "What did you do to

rattle his cage like that?" She asked. I took a long breath. When I told Sam and Cheryl about how I failed as a potential knight in the army of King Arthur they both laughed.

"Geeks!" Cheryl waved her hand. "I swear sometimes I wish I could spank some sense into them."

"Somebody should explain to him that not all of us want to play dungeons and dragons," Said Samantha, shrugging her shoulders as she sat back down.

Car Pool

THIS MORNING ON the bus I watched a woman apply makeup. It
was truly a feat of determination. She held a compact mirror in her
left hand, a mascara wand in the right. Sitting down, she placed
both hands ready in the ideal position for application. As we snaked
around the city she swayed back and forth with the motion of the
bus, waiting for a brief moment of stillness. As soon as the bus
stopped to let on passengers, she would dab a few smears of mascara
on her eye lashes and stop again right before the bus started moving.
It's as if she could anticipate the bus's movements ahead of time and
react to its jolts and jerks intuitively. I watched her apply mascara,
eye liner and lipstick using the same marvellous method. A small
miracle unfolding right before my eyes. Watching it was
exhilarating.

It reminded me of the excitement I felt the day Ismail moved in with me. I know it sounds silly, but I actually dressed up and applied makeup that day. I wore skinny jeans and a fuchsia top that showed off my boobs when worn on top of my push-up bra. I even styled my hair. I wanted Ismail's first day with me to be remarkable. I cleaned the apartment thoroughly and made room for his things in my closet. He had so few clothes and yet I cleared out half my closet for him. I wanted to show him that I was making room for him in my life. And then he showed up with five boxes of books and a suitcase. The books he stacked in his half of closet and then he hung up his few clothes. Aside from books he brought three old cracked plates, a cup, a mug and a tea kettle. Moving him in was seamless. There was just one snag. One little hiccup. He told me that he couldn't live in a place where there was a TV in the sitting room. He unplugged my prized 40 inch plasma flat screen set and placed it on top of his books in the closet where it would be out of sight. I objected. "But my insomnia! I need the TV for my insomnia." Ismail stood in the middle of my living room and adopted the stance and voice of an infomercial celebrity.

"Ladies and gentlemen, boys and girls, listen up! Today, for the very first time I will share with you my amazing discovery. After years of long research and tireless questing, I would like to present to you a pill that will make you happy, improve your sex life, make you look great and change your life forever. This is a one-time special offer of a radical patent pending discovery of Ismail's miracle pill. Normally a one-month supply would set you back 300 dollars, but for you, my dear and loyal audience, I will offer you one month

completely free of charge! Yes, you heard that right—absolutely free. All you have to do is listen carefully and follow the instructions to get your hands on this unique opportunity to obtain true happiness.

Oh, I know what you are thinking. You are thinking 'this is too good to be true, if Ismail had the miracle pill why would he be sharing it with me for free? Either he should be using it to make himself a millionaire, or the 'miracle pill' simply doesn't work.' Well I can understand your skepticism. I have been stung by false or exaggerated advertising before, but believe me this is no spam offer promising to enlarge your body parts. No, no, this that I offer you today is the real thing. I know, I know—you have been promised happiness before only to be disappointed.

"Let me explain," said Ismail, dropping the smooth infomercial voice and becoming himself again.

I remember a soap commercial that aired when I was a kid. A man is in the shower using a particular bar of soap, and when he turns around you see a tiny man surfing on his back, between his shoulder blades. I told my mom that I wanted to buy the soap that would make that surfing man appear on my back. I was shocked to discover that there was no such thing. I later made my mother buy me that particular brand of soap to verify for myself that it wasn't true. It made me smell nice, but no mini surfing man.

And there was the commercial that showed women having an orgasm while using Herbal Essence shampoo in the shower. Look at the happy satisfied woman who has just used the shampoo! This is an insult to manhood. If a woman can be this satisfied after using shampoo, why would any woman need a man?

It began to dawn on me that there was something wrong when my friend and I were watching a TV program together one day. We would chat during a commercial break, and as soon as the program would come on both of us would stop in mid conversation and go back to watching the screen Shouldn't I be finding my buddy more interesting than *The Walking Dead*?

And then I called my friend one day for a chat, and he said that his favorite show was on. He couldn't talk to me right then because she was watching *Friends*. I thought to myself: "Wouldn't you rather talk to a real friend, that really cares about you and is a real person, than watching your pretend friends?"

All these things were swirling around in the back of my mind. And then I went to see the movie *Manufacturing Consent*. Shortly afterwards I took my TV and locked it in the closet in my bedroom.

People frequently wonder how I have time to work full time, help others, be an activist and maintain an active social life. The answer is simple, I don't own a TV set. I have to use my own imagination to entertain myself.

I don't sit around watching a hockey match. If I feel in a sporty mood, I go out for a run, or I go kayaking, or hiking or whatever else strikes my fancy. After getting rid of my TV, being the couch potato became boring, so I had to get moving.

My dear Car, you don't need generic entertainment for the masses manufactured to perpetuate the corrupt capitalist system. You have this!" Ismail said, gesturing to his body. "I will satisfy every need you can possibly think of. I will tell you stories before going to

bed, straight from my imagination, and then dazzle you with mind blowing sex.

I haven't owned a TV set for six years. Most people are surprised when I tell them that. Here are some of the responses I got from different people:

So what do you do in the evenings before you go to bed? You sit around reading a book? Hahahaha, that must be so boring.

Is that for religious reasons? Do you belong to some kind of a cult?

If you don't watch TV, you will become a social outcast for not having the same cultural references that your peers do.

I can't live without my Seinfeld.

But you look like a normal person!

"Anyway I have been rambling," said Ismail, who once again adopted his infomercial host persona. "And you are just dying to know how to get your hands on those miracle pills. All you have to do is follow these simple instructions and a one month supply of Ismail's miracle pills will arrive by mail absolutely free.

1. Turn off your TV for two weeks. No TV viewing allowed.

2. Spend time with people you like during the same two week interval.

3. Take yourself out for a date at least once on each week. All you have to do is go out and do something that you really enjoy. It might be going to see a show, going for a walk, visiting an art gallery or dining in a fine restaurant. It doesn't matter what, as long as it is something you enjoy.

If you follow these instructions religiously, your free supply of pills will arrive shortly thereafter. How will Ismail know that you have followed the instructions? Because Big Ismail is watching you. He will know!"

After that performance, how could I resist? I smiled suggestively and next thing I knew I was lying on the floor of the living room on my way to bliss. I gave up TV and in return was promised personalized storytelling followed by fantastic sex. I can hear you asking ..... *Well? Did he deliver?* Oh Boy did he ever! All that stereotypical nonsense about Arab men being good in bed, well, it turns out it's not nonsense at all. This one has its roots in reality.

So now the TV is sitting in my closet and every once in a while I feel the temptation to plug it back in. Like right now. But then I feel like that would be admitting defeat, acknowledging that I am sad, lonely and bored. Next bus stop, I will start collecting cats and become the pathetic cat lady. I think instead I need to put energy into the second point on my heartbreak healing project plan. Reconnect with old friends and make new friends. Since most of our friends were really Ismail's friends, Our separation left me poor in the social group department. I really miss my pre-Ismail friends Bianca and Judy. We used to be the mighty trio. We went clubbing and partying together. We had so much fun. And then we drifted

apart. It's not like we had a falling out or anything, It's just that we saw each other less and less until we didn't see each other at all. I have been thinking about reconnecting now for weeks but I don't know how. It seems needy to come out of the blue and say *Hey, now that I am divorced, lets hang out together.* I need to find a way to take a first step without seeming desperate. I met Judy in second year in university. She had a car and since we lived in the neighbourhood she would offer me rides whenever our schedules overlapped. Chatting in the car led to the bursts of laughter and fits of giggles until we turned to best friends. I met Bianca in grade 12 in North West High. She is the most sincere and most down to earth person I ever met. We had our first drink of alcohol together. Consoled each other through our first heart breaks. After much effort to psych myself up, I wrote each of them a simple message through Facebook suggesting we meet at local bar for drinks at a time that would suit both of them. After I hit the send button, I could feel my heart pounding. Exhilaration at the idea of reconnecting with them, and fear of rejection. Maybe they wouldn't want anything to do with me.

Speaking of rejection, today was the day for it. Chris asked to see what I had written so far in my Excalibur user documentation. I happily sent him the first three chapters. Introduction, Installation and Configuration. I thought that he would be impressed that I had figured out what the software does all on my own. Without asking him to explain anything. Ten minutes after hitting the send button, I could hear Chris's bulldozer steps rumbling down the cube farm,

radiating his rage across the field. I braced myself for impact. Chris felt no need to put brakes on his feelings; he just started screaming.

"You are ruining my work! You are destroying everything." He was waving his hands around and shaking his head so much that I worried he might be having a seizure.

"It's only a start, I've only been working on it for one day," I said calmly.

"Too stupid. Don't understand. Wrong start. No direction. Disaster end." He was in such a frenzy he had lost the ability to form whole sentences. At this point his face turned red and he looked like he had trouble breathing. He was opening and closing his mouth like a fish gulping air instead of water. Who knew that Chris could display so much passion? In a moment of crazy panic, I found myself uttering words I thought I would never say.

"Relax, Chris! It's just user documentation. Everyone knows nobody reads the user documentation anyway."

Chris turned pale white. One last big gulp of air was consumed. He shook his head, Turned around and walked back to his desk.

One second later both Sam and Cheryl were at my desk offering me hugs and words of consolation. I tried to brush it off, but then I got a text message from Yuri.

I had a nice time with you the other day. See each other again? Please trim bush next time ... lol

How am I supposed to respond to that? "Go have sex with an inflatable doll instead?" "Yes I promise to alter my private parts for your amusement?" I wish he had blown me off instead. Or sent me a

rude rejection. It's not like his performance in bed was that great anyway. Say what you like about Ismail, he always had a positive attitude about my body. Bush or no bush, I gained weight or lost weight. My hair was long or short, it didn't matter. He loved it all. He always seemed to appreciate having access to my naked body, no matter the state it was in. With him there was no shame. I could let loose and feel confident being naked. He looked at me as if I was a goddess. That text message was the last straw. I went to the women's toilet to have a little cry in private. Then I washed my face and went back to work.

Now you would think that would be the worst of it, Right? I mean what else could possibly go wrong in a single 9-5 day? A few minutes after I had returned to my desk, Ron came over and sat in the visitor chair in my cubicle. Ron is the man who sits in the office next to Chris. He sighed deeply and rubbed his hands as if he was preparing himself to shovel a deep hole.

Finally, he said: "I need to tell you something that is delicate. You have to promise me not to share this information with anybody."

Like a fool I nodded, agreeing to keep the secret, but not knowing what it was.

"Chris is my best friend in the world," he said. "Technically he is my boss, but he is like a brother. Right now, he is having a difficult time. I am not going to burden you with all the details, but he has health issues. Heart trouble. It is quite serious. Don't be alarmed. He is seeing a doctor and receiving treatment. His delicate situation requires him to stay calm. Any agitation might bring about

a heart attack. The medication he is on isn't helping much in the staying calm department. It seems to be making him all sensitive and emotional. Now I know he seems like a strong man, but believe me he is all delicate broken china on the inside right now. I am here to besiege you to be gentle and sensitive with him. I know I have no right to be asking you this, but I am hoping to appeal to your grace."

I told Ron that I was sorry to hear that Chris had health problems, but it was him who had been rude to me. I asked Ron to ask him to cool down the shouting and hysterics.

"Yes! Of course. I know! I will talk to him," said Ron. "I am not putting this on you at all. I am just hoping you will help me out to save my best friend. I would appreciate it; I would be in your debt. I owe you one."

Well, what could I say? Of course I promised to do whatever I could to keep Chris calm. So now I have this extra heavy luggage in my trunk: *Make sure that Chris doesn't drop dead in the office because of me.* Yay, me!

As he was leaving, Ron laid another ton of bricks on me. "You know, Car, the bunch of us on Excalibur play this game where we pretend to be the knights of the round table at Camelot. It keeps the work environment fun. When Chris asked you to prove your worth, he was actually inviting you to be a member of the team. You should have felt honored. It was a playful gesture. Instead he received a dressing down from the VP of Engineering. That hurt his pride."

And now I am sitting in my apartment staring at my laptop feeling all the layers of rejection the day had to offer. I am acutely feeling the pain of missing Ismail. I wish I could jump in his arms and get him to tell me one of his stories. Do I have the determination to get through this without becoming a bitter, angry person? Yes I do. Yes I do. For inspiration I visualize the woman on the bus applying her mascara, and keep telling myself *I will be alright! I am shit right now. But I will emerge out of this one day somehow.*

One good thing happened today. I received a package in the mail from Sylvester. In it I found a leather handbag in white, brown and black. It came with a note: "Every urban explorer needs a trusty hand bag to carry the necessities you need to take care of yourself. Make sure to fill this bag with whatever you need to keep yourself comfortable along the way."

Motion Sickness

THIS MORNING THERE were too many people on the bus. Everybody was squeezed in against each other. When the windows steamed up, a drop of condensation trickled down my neck. I spent the rest of the bus trip wondering what that liquid was. Distilled snot? Condensed sweat? Maybe it came from me? Maybe it came from somebody who is no longer on the bus? A leftover body moisture. I studied the faces of the people on the bus one by one, searching for a suspect. The dark skinned young man with goatee looks so earnest, it couldn't be him. The sloppy millennial with blue hair and a pierced lip. If this was a detective novel, she would be the obvious suspect and therefore it wouldn't be her. It would be somebody that nobody suspected at the very beginning. The middle age white man in a business suit. He looks out of place. He looks

like somebody who would be commuting to work in his custom made Jaguar. What is he doing on this bus? Perhaps his Jag broke down and he is forced to lower his standards by riding with the rest of us. But he doesn't look annoyed. I wouldn't say he is amused, however he lacks the irritation that you would expect in a patron of the public transit system given his stature. I shouldn't leap to conclusions before I have examined the rest of my companions on this temporary ride. This Chinese middle-aged woman. She looks weary. Like it's only the beginning of the day and already she has had enough ...... Oh, the mystery won't be solved. The bus has arrived at my destination without me deciding on a guilty party.

All I remember from my wedding day is how nervous I was. It was supposed to be the happiest day of my life, but I passed through it like a high-speed race and crossed the finish line a married woman. I had a small wedding. We didn't want to spend money and so we had a picnic in the park. All I cared about was the dress. I wanted to look beautiful in my wedding dress. I bought a knee high A-line white dress that had laser-cut flowers attached at random locations. I had one frilly flower sticking out exactly at my right hip. The whole day, my hand was swiping against it until the fabric flower got scrunched up and frayed along the edges. Another flower found its happy location on top of my butt crack. It looked like it

was growing out of my asshole. "Why did I like this at the shop?" I thought to myself as I looked in the mirror of my bedroom on my special day. At the shop I had felt daring in the dress. On the day that mattered I just felt ridiculous. How could my perceptions have fooled me so dramatically?

With Ismail came access to a car. He owned a dark blue second hand Toyota. It was nothing special and Ismail didn't regard it with any particular care. To him it was the most practical means of transportation. Marriage comes with many benefits that nobody tells you about. Sex on demand. You can gloriously have sex whenever you want without all the hassle of going out, meeting, mingling and dating. There is also the built-in companionship. Anytime you want to go for a walk and chat with somebody there is somebody right there that you can do it with. It's actually a fantastic thing. My marriage came with an extra perk—access to a car. There is something about a marriage certificate that gives you the feeling that you own what your spouse owns. It's a fantastic feeling. One month into our marriage, past midnight, Ismail was snoring next to me. I couldn't sleep. I got out of bed and Tiptoed to the living room where I changed into black sweat pants and a black top. I grabbed Ismail's keys off the table counter and slipped out of the apartment and into his car. Our car. Although I don't have a driver's licence, it's very rare that you are required to produce it. My heart was beating like a clunky engine as I turned the key in the ignition. And there I was driving in a car which I technically owned. Driving like a little old grandmother around the block three times gave me the confidence to pick up speed and venture farther away. I heard the

words of Martin Luther King in my ear: "Free at last, Free at last, Thank God almighty we are free at last." There are moments in life that are so beautiful and so perfect that they make you want to believe in a supreme creator. That first night, I didn't dare put on the radio, I was too absorbed by the sensations of movement in my body. The sound of the engine reverberated in my soul. The whooshing sound my wheels made against the wet asphalt of the street was a new form of poetry. The fading sounds of a city past midnight, an orchestra with each member tuning their instrument preparing to play. A distant car honk here. A nearby flash of a headlight. The city sparkled with lights, hazy fumes and the occasional lazy pedestrian toddling along. Dawn was right around the corner but it was hard to sense that at that particular hour. One hour later I tiptoed back into my bed. Ismail was breathing deeply and rhythmically on his side of the bed. I remember how happy that moment was. No! It wasn't happiness. It was contentment. I was deeply contented. I remember saying: "Thank god for Ismail" under my breath. I wanted to kiss him on the forehead, but I was too afraid of waking him. You would never think that a tender wholesome moment would lead you into the pit of darkness a few years later.

At work today, Chris came over to yell at me some more. Boom! Back to reality.

"This is the single worst documentation I have ever read. This is even worse than the documentation where you read a single line and think to yourself: Ok then! This must have been written in China." His face puffed up and turned red.

I took a deep breath in, then a deep breath out and said nothing. Amazingly, Chris paused as if he was waiting for me to say something. He looked like an idling car.

"At least the written in China documentation doesn't mislead people. This is worse," he said, stabbing the piece of paper he was holding with his finger, "because people will actually read it and believe what it says."

"I have heard of fake news, but this is the first time I've seen fake user documentation." He stopped punching the paper and turned pale white. His breathing became shallow and fast. I worried that he was about to have a heart attack. I jumped out of my swivel chair, pulled out the guest chair in my cubicle and instructed Christ to sit on it. In a soothing voice I repeated: "Calm down Chris. Breathe! Breathe! It's just documentation. It doesn't matter."

Cheryl popped her head over the cubicle divider, concerned. I asked her to get Chris a glass of water. She went running to the kitchen. Sam walked over and asked if she should dial 911. I shook my head no. Chris looked like he was enjoying all the attention. He drank his glass of water and continued breathing as if he was in a Lamaze class. Gradually a more natural color returned to his cheeks.

"Thank you!" his voice was soft. "I feel better."

"Good," I said, surprised that Chris was actually approving something I had done.

"You need to change this documentation," he whispered in between short breaths.

"I will happily change it," I said. "Just write me a detailed email with corrections and I will get started on the changes right away." Yes! Cooperation at last.

He jumped out of his seat and started yelling.

"I don't have time for this shit! You are asking me to do your job for you! Just do your job right and stop harassing me." He turned around and stomped away towards his desk.

Sam, Cheryl and I just stared at each other. I looked at Cheryl. She looked at Sam. Sam looked at me. All of us shrugged our shoulders at the same time. All three of us went back to our computer terminals to get our work done.

In the evening I had a first date with Joshua. He said that meeting in a coffee shop was lame so I got into a taxi to meet him in a bar at the other side of the town.

"The light this time of the day is really bothering my eyes. That's why I'm wearing these dark glasses," said the taxi driver as I was getting into the back seat.

"Yes, I guess there is a bit of a glare." I didn't particularly like the idea that my taxi driver couldn't see where he is going.

"I hope it will be better when I have my cataract surgery in a few months," he said. "I can hardly see out of my right eye." He started the car and drove off into the oncoming traffic.

"Oh!" The worry fuel level was going up in my worry tank.

"Don't worry! I can get you to your destination safely. I know the streets of this city like the palm of my hand." He wobbled his head right to left to emphasize the point.

"Except most people don't really know the palm of their hand," I said. Me and my stupid logical thinking.

"It's just an expression. I can drive this car with my eyes shut! Look! Look! My eyes are shut! Do you notice any difference in my driving?" He flung his head back so that I could see in the rear-view mirror that his eyes were shut behind the dark glasses.

"Please keep you eyes open!" The worry tank had overflowed. I was now panicking.

"Not until you answer my question." A faint smile appeared on his face. The bastard was enjoying this.

"Oh God! We're going to crash!" I covered my face with my hands.

"Don't panic, lady! You need to trust more. Just answer the question, "he said, his smile widening. I wanted to punch him in the back of the head.

"What's the question again?" See how sensible I am.

"Do you notice any difference in my driving?" He was gesturing with his right hand as if conducting an opera. You already know how much I hate the opera.

"No, your driving is fantastic. Now please open your eyes." Threaten me with death and I will say anything you want me to say.

"Ok! See! My eyes are open and I am driving exactly the same way. It's because we taxi drivers have a different brain," He said, his right hand swooping right to left as if he was a rapper.

"Different brain? What does that even mean?" I regretted the question right after saying it. It was a trap.

"We have taxi brain. It has been proven by science. The sensible people who designed North American cities like New York had the brilliant idea of building roads in a grid. A taxi driver can navigate effectively to any street corner on their first day. London, now, that's another story. That place is a confusing mix of random street names in an even more random orientations such that even an intrepid explorer like me gets hopelessly lost. As a result, to become a Taxi Driver in London you have to pass a test. This brutal examination, called 'The Knowledge', requires the memorization of around 25,000 streets and 20,000 landmarks within 6 miles of Charing Cross station. Now, if you're like me, you're thinking 'easy enough, I could knock that out in a couple of weeks.' Shockingly though, it tends to take the average Joe 2-4 years to pass the test!

The taxi driver's brain is special. I practically have a GPS system implanted in my head. It's like a super power."

My super hero taxi driver paused waiting for applause or perhaps comments of adoration. Just to spite him I said absolutely nothing.

"You probably think you have a much better memory than a London taxi drivers, but scientific evidence says that's not the case. A while ago, a group of neuroscientists chucked some taxi drivers into a fancy scanner so they could compare their brains to those of regular folk.

My bet is they wanted to see if there was a brain defect that was causing the drivers to put themselves through the horrific examination. However, the findings were much more surprising! Over their 2-4 years of training, taxi drivers actually showed a significant increase in the size of a part of their brain called the hippocampus, which turns out to play a role in spatial navigation. See, taxi drivers flex this little brain muscle enough, and it boosts their navigational powers. And that's not all! Their hippocampuses kept on expanding after the test!

But there's good news...you know what I am about to say? Right?"

He paused again, hoping I would urge him to continue. I gave him more of the silent treatment.

"There is one teeny thing, though. Although modifying your brain structure by preparing for a test seems pretty amazing, it isn't all good news. Only some parts of the hippocampus increased in size. Other parts shrank. Otherwise your brain would explode, right? There's only so much room in your skull. So what were the taxi drivers sacrificing during their training period? My guess is it's

probably their sense of humor. That would explain why nobody gets any of my jokes." Clearly he had rehearsed this speech. I bet he thought it made him sound clever.

"But we aren't in London, so that means that your brain isn't that special," I said, looking out the window and trying to keep my mind off the fact that I was being driven by a blind taxi driver.

"I lived in London ten years ago. That means my brain is double special. I learned the map of London plus the map of our beautiful city as well. You get the double special taxi driver service today. I think you should pay double, but don't worry, I won't insist on that." I guess that must be more of his fantastic humor that I am supposed to laugh at.

I exited the taxi grateful to be still alive. I stood on the street corner and said a little prayer. "Thank you God for letting me survive that ride! I was convicted I was about to die. "

I straightened out my jacket and entered the pub. Loud heavy metal music slapped me in the face. *I have a feeling I am not going to like this guy,* I thought to myself as I plowed through the masses of people. People were pushing me out of the way so I had to squeeze through and push back in order to find Joshua. I scanned the place and found him, at the far left corner of the bar sitting all by himself. I recognized his face from his profile picture. I waded my way through the crowds and said hello, and just in case he couldn't hear me over all the noise I also waved my hand and smiled. Joshua jumped out of his seat and gave me a big bear hug. It felt a bit weird but I went with it. We couldn't hear each other. I would shout. He would shout. But no communication was happening. And so we

settled to smiles and gestures. And looking at each other awkwardly. He had long brown hair and had a silver earning dangling from his right ear lobe, and his black leather vest made him look like a member of a heavy metal band.

I ordered a gin and tonic. He drank several beers. I stopped counting after eight. It occurred to me that he very likely had a drug problem. After about two hours of looking and smiling at each other, I got up and mimed that I was going home by pointing at my wrist and the exit sign. Joshua smiled, nodded his head to indicate that he understood, got out of his seat and gave me a kiss on the cheek. I walked out feeling relieved. Another day was almost over. I still had the bus drive back to my apartment to contend with. I walked out the bar hoping that the bus driver was possessed with the gift of eyesight.

Side Mirror

A MORBIDLY OBESE woman got on the bus midway through my ride to work. Her voice reverberated inside my eardrums before her substantial girth blessed the inside of the vehicle. "Wait! It will take me a while to get on," she yelled at the bus driver in whiny shrieks that pierced the air the way earrings penetrate earlobes. Then she proceeded to grunt as she pulled on the the door handles and heaved her weight onto the vehicle: "Eh! eh! eh! eh!" She went on and on. This must be what a live whale beaching looks like. A member of "The Vulnerables" for sure, is about to make an appearance. I was standing, holding onto pole, staring out the foggy window and pretending to ignore the action taking place. No sooner did her feet land on the bus floor, than she accosted three seated people: "Please let me sit, my feet are hurting, I need to sit." All three jumped out

of their seats and joined the standing masses. She let out a long and hearty sigh as she sat down. Her sense of relief lightened the air from the rear to the front of the vehicle. Everybody around me jostled by doing a little shuffly dance eager to resume normalcy without further interruption.

Across from the fat lady sat a stick-thin young Korean woman who was taking turns looking into a map and looking out the window to catch a glimpse of street signs. A young man sitting next to the Korean woman leaned towards her and asked her in the softest kindest voice you could possibly imagine: "Are you lost? Do you need any help?" She answered him in shattered English.

"Aaaaaaaaaaa! yes!" She said after a pause. "Looking .... Community?" She pointed a dainty little finger onto her map.

"Are you looking for the community center?" The man asked.

"Aaaaaa .... yes .....no......yes!" She placed her hand over her mouth as if holding in a gasp.

"Show me on the map where you would like to go," said Mr. Nice Guy.

"Aaaaaaaaaaa!" She said. That must be how Koreans register confusion.

The young man gestured towards the map. "Map. Show me where you are going." Ever so helpful.

The young woman stared at her map looking even more confused. "Yes, this my map." She spread out the map across her lap.

The young man smiled widely. "Yes, this is your map." More nodding.

"Need street." Finally she said something useful!

"Do you know the name of the street?"

"Wha?" I presume she meant 'what?'

"Street name." Mr. Nice Guy was cajoling an answer like a vacuum cleaner seeks dust.

"Aha!" Well! At least she didn't say "Aaaaaaaaaaaaaa" again. That would be annoying.

"For example, Broadway, Granville, Burrard, Smithe...."

"Yes, yes Smitty!" She interrupted him, excitedly waving her finger up and down.

"Smithe Street, is that the street you want?" I never saw a man so happy saying a street name.

No doubt her pretty face and youthful looks were making it easier for Mr. Nice Guy to be so patient.

"Aaaaaaaaaa! Smity ...... community."

The obese woman had been watching this interaction attentively with eyes darting left to right the whole time, as if she was watching a tennis match. Then she interjected, yelling:

"Shut up already! I can't stand hearing you mangle English anymore."

The Korean woman opened her mouth and stared at the obese lady, as if in shock. Then she looked down with tears welling in her eyes. She placed a fragile quivering hand on her right cheek. The young man stared as well, looking stunned. It took him a few seconds to gather his thoughts, but finally he said: "This doesn't concern you, she was talking to me."

"She doesn't know where she is going, just let her get lost, that will teach her a lesson," the obese woman said in her whiny, high pitched voice.

"Haven't you ever been a foreigner in a foreign country?" Mr. Nice Guy, asked.

"No!" She shook her head right and left to the maximum that her thick neck would allow.

"Well I have, and I have always appreciated it when people helped me out when I was lost."

The obese lady stood up and stared screaming: "I can't take this anymore. Everybody is mean to me. Bus driver, bus driver, stop right now! I need to get off!" The speed with which she got up was in sharp contrast to the effort it had taken her to sit down.

The bus driver stopped immediately, even though they're not supposed to do that. The obese lady huffed and puffed herself off the bus making whiny noises the entire time.

I wish I could have advised the obese lady to apply her talents towards becoming an opera singer. For one, her unique girth would fit the stereotype. Plus, she would get paid for heaping abuse on other people. Heavy shrieking and whining is encouraged in that profession.

Some people take up so much room. I am not talking about physical space, but requiring attention, being needy.

Clearly the obese lady hadn't experienced a young man (or any man?) giving her soft attention very frequently. The Korean woman was everything the Obese woman was not: beautiful, healthy, exotic and desirable. I don't know if I feel revulsion or sympathy for the

obese woman. An obese lady is an easy target. The easiest thing is to yell back: "Shut up, Fatso!" I try not to be judgmental, but some people just invite judgement. They might as well wear a giant sign around their necks that says: "Please judge me."

After our third date, I told Ismail that *Casablanca* was my favorite movie in the whole wide world. "Never heard of it," was his reply. So I invited him over to my apartment for dinner. The plan was to eat dinner and watch the movie together. I was hoping that the romance in the movie would lead to sex in my bedroom. It was the first time I had cooked for Ismail, and I felt nervous. I am not much of a cook. I decided to go the extra mile and cook something special, which was my first mistake. I decided to make a traditional Portuguese dish called rojões de porco—a type of a pork stew my mother made. I phoned up my mother and got her to describe the recipe to me in detail, which she gladly did. She even offered to make the dish for me and deliver it to my apartment, but I refused. I wanted to cook for Ismail with my own hands. I even went to my mother's speciality grocery store across the town to get the same exact brand of red paprika that she buys. I paired it with saffron rice, garden salad and black olives.

Right off the bat, I could tell that Ismail hated the food. He took one bite out of the stew and then ate mostly the rice and salad.

When I asked him if there was something wrong with the food, he said: "I am not a big fan of pork." A year later I learned that all Moroccans hate pork. This was absolutely the worst dish I would have cooked for Ismail.

Then we settled on my couch, and I popped *Casablanca* into the DVD player. Halfway through, Ismail said: "I am sorry, I can't watch any more of this."

"But the best part is yet to come!" I said.

"This movie is unbearably racist," he said. "I'm surprised that an intelligent lady like you finds it romantic. Did you not notice how Moroccan people are depicted in this colonialist trash?" Then he proceeded to lecture me about all the crimes that the French committed in North Africa, including Morocco. He complained how the movie depicts European yearning for liberation, yet completely ignores that Morocco was under French colonial rule at the same time. The evening was a disaster. Ismail stormed out of my apartment and I thought I would never see him again. A few days later he called to apologize. We both apologized to each other. I promised to destroy my DVD of *Casablanca* and never watch it again and he promised to be calmer in his objections the next time. He told me he would show me one of his favorite movies called *The Battle of Algiers,* which he described as the movie that exposes what a lie the movie *Casablanca* is. And he told me he would cook real food for me, not those chicken scraps I made for him.

Perhaps that dinner at my house should have been a clue. My head said:

Don't fall in love because he has a nice smile.

Don't trust the guy with a nice smile that calls your cooking chicken scraps.

Don't go to another date with the guy after he angrily stormed out of your apartment, leaving you to cry yourself to sleep.

Don't go see the man who says you are not his type. The man who tells you he likes either blondes or women with black hair, and that brunettes are too middle of the road for his liking.

Don't make decisions on a smile when the smile is attached to a man who waits three days before he calls to apologize for his rude behavior.

My head was screaming at me. Shouting! I didn't listen. Off I went to see him again. What a stupid dumb brainless chicken I was.

I hereby resolve to learn from my mistakes. Sigh! Onwards and upwards.

The first thing I did when I arrived at the office this morning was write a rejection message to Joshua. You have no idea how difficult this was. I had to psych myself up to do it. I actually talked out loud to myself: "You can do it. Just do it. Say no. You know it's the right thing." I waved my hands around to get rid of some of the negative energy and then I exhaled deeply and went straight to my keyboard to do the deed.

Dear Joshua,

It was very nice meeting you last night. I had a good time. However, I don't think we are a good match. Good luck on the dating scene for the both of us.

Have a fantastic day,

Car

I hit the send button and exhaled deeply. The trick is to do the whole thing while holding my breath, so that I don't loose my nerve. Now I just have to wait for the abuse to shower over my head. Most men feel compelled to reply with something nasty. And don't forget the daily shouting shower that rains on my head from Chris.

The day wasn't a complete waste. Two good things happened. The first is that Stephanie called me into her office and told me that I had been selected to go to The Technical Writer's Conference held in San Francisco. This made me very happy. I was expecting Cheryl to be selected since she is more senior. I see this as a vote of confidence. I discussed the daily shouting session with Stephanie. She was very sympathetic and understanding. "I am aware of the situation and I am in discussions with the R&D manager. It's a delicate situation. Thank you for your understanding." That made me so happy I skipped back to my chair.

Later that evening I had a long overdue get together with Bianca and Judy. After a lengthy Facebook exchange, Bianca had chosen the Dockside Lounge at the Wedgewood Hotel, a swanky upscale place for our gathering. I arrived fashionably late—15 minutes—and yet I was there first. All three of us screamed with joy upon seeing each other. Judy is married and has a daughter. Bianca is still dating Emerson. The same Emerson she met in college. To

my great relief we didn't spend the whole evening talking about my divorce and what a sad a pathetic person I am. Instead we spent a good chunk of the evening talking about what Bianca needed to do to get Emerson to propose, Judy taking the lead as she always does in all matters involving handling a man. I suppose in our trio she is the alpha female. She has a diamond ring on her finger and cute baby pictures on her cell phone. Bianca is the mid-range female on the social dominance hierarchy, since at least she has a potential husband in the works. I am at very bottom of this prestige ladder, with a failed marriage under my belt and no real prospects. The strategies we considered to get Bianca walking down the aisle: give him an ultimatum, make him jealous by giving attention to other men, or just drop hints. We discussed the pros and cons of each option and how they could misfire. When I got home I felt sad. Being around Judy and Bianca reminded me of what I was like a few years back. I was a happy, enthusiastic woman with infinite potential. And look at me now. I went to bed, but I couldn't sleep. I kept tossing and turning. "I wish Ismail was here to tell me a story," I thought to myself with each readjustment in my bed. One side. The other side. On my back. On my tummy. Around and around I went. His stories had done the trick with my insomnia.

Mustang

THE SO CALLED ADVANCED nations became advanced at the expense of other nations. How did Holland become Holland? By colonizing Indonesia, South Africa and other countries. By murdering, exploiting and pillaging. Compare life today in Indonesia to life in Holland. The difference is the result of colonization. How did Britain become what it is today? By colonizing India, Iraq, Zimbabwe and many others. By exploiting the resources of others and killing millions who stood in the way of their imperial ambitions. Compare life today in India versus life in the UK. That is what colonization has accomplished. Westerners carry themselves with an air of superiority pretending that they uphold values of equality, democracy and humanity. The West is superior in only one way. Building weapons that can devastate millions and using this

savage power to push their interests above all else. Laurence of Arabia is a lie. To the West he might seem like a hero but to us he is the worst of villains.

This was Ismail's standard speech. I was at the receiving end of it at least ten times. This was something he was certain about. His stance on this was non-negotiable. The way he pursed his lips when delivering the treatise, the way he stuck all the fingers in his right hand together until his fist formed a tear shape made clear to me that I had better act the rapt audience. This knowledge empowered him. Gave him a place in the world. Which makes me think of things that empower men in general.

The 1963 Ford Mustang was my father's car. In an unusual act of rebellion, he drove home with it without consulting my mom, having bought it from a guy he met in a bar. In an incredible turn of events, my mother didn't make much of fuss—as dad jumped out of the red vehicle beaming a victorious smile towards the world. This was the ride of somebody who was going somewhere. This was the stuff of dreams turning into reality. This was the man version of Cinderella watching a pumpkin turn into a carriage. Mom walked out and inhaled. Before she had a chance to say anything, dad glided over, held her by both forearms and planted a wet kiss on her cheek. Mom exhaled and said nothing. The words dissolved into his manly

confidence. That kiss was the most erotic thing I have ever seen in my life. Physically it was no different from hundreds of kisses on the cheek I saw my father dispatch. It was the effect this one kiss had. The way it rendered my mother speechless and made her act out of character—it was a high octane kiss. Later that day both my parents spent a long time in the bedroom behind a locked door. At the time I had no idea what they were doing there, but I think I know now. Albert and I admired the shiny metal and felt compelled to touch every nook and cranny of the new purchase. This was not a practical car for a family of four. With only two doors and cramped backseats, my brother and I had to squeeze through each time to get in. A booster seat was placed in the back for Albert for the longest time, until he outgrew it. One Sunday afternoon my mother was washing dishes in the kitchen, Al was playing with his toy cars, making vroom vroom sounds. Dad put down his newspaper. The crumpling sound went woosh woosh as he folded it next to his chair. He looked straight at me and whispered: "Hey! Would you like to go for a ride?" I nodded yes. We both snuck out without making much noise. I got into the passenger seat for the first time. Feeling a bit guilty to be taking my mother's place, I wiggled my bottom into the ribbed seating to make the most out the opportunity. As dad drove out of the driveway, I reached my hand towards the radio dial to turn it on, but dad told me not to. "I want you to listen to the symphony of this car's engine," he said in his Portuguese accent. "Listen to the firing order. The wide torque band allows the car to put on a performance as we speed up. Listen to the exhaust sound. The long pull to the second gear. The

suspension, the brakes, the engine, the manual transmission all interact together to give me constant feedback. A fun interactive ride like no other. You can't get this in a Ferrari. I am creating my own music as I drive this car. I am the maestro." I didn't understand everything he said, but I listened to that deep throaty engine sound like it was the first alien signal to arrive to planet Earth. I asked my dad why he chose the red, and he corrected me: "It isn't red, it's Rangoon red." Rangoon is the former name of the capital city of Burma. I didn't know that either. For the longest time I thought that Rangoon was a deep metallic shade of red. From that day on, that rumbling engine sound called out to me. I would be sitting on the orange faux suede couch in our third floor apartment. At first I would hear a faint buzz that would increase in volume until it was rhythmic pounding whir which got amplified into that familiar doppler wail. That sound that indicated that somebody I loved had just come home.

Most Sundays I would catch my father outside washing and cleaning his car. He started by shampooing and rinsing the car. Then he would hand dry it with a special towel. Then he would turn his attention to cleaning the inside. Out came the floor mats. The upholstery was cleaned by hand. The floor received attention with the hand held vacuum cleaner. Every square inch of that car was lovingly touched by my father's hands. Most people couldn't believe that car was bought second hand. It always looked shiny and clean. It smelled like freshly laundered sheets. We weren't allowed to eat or drink inside the car.

And then the fabric of my life got shredded into tatters when my father, Emilio Franka, died suddenly. A hit and run. He was walking home holding a grocery bag that contained 2 liters of milk and a bag of cheese puffs. My father lay in a pool of milk with swirls of blood in it. Neon orange cheese puffs dotted the whole scene. He died two hours later at the hospital. "The driver was probably drunk," the police officer said to my mother. The person responsible for my father's death was never caught.

I felt sad, but mostly I felt angry. It was a reminder that anything can be taken away from you any minute, and when you least expect it. After his death everything that belonged to my father gained a special significance. His favorite chair. His clothes. And most importantly his car. I laid my claim to the Mustang and my mother promised me that I could drive it as soon as I had my driving license. The first time I failed my driving test, my mother said: "Everybody fails their first one." The second time she said: "Don't worry you will pass the next one." The third time she didn't say anything. She just nodded her head and grunted. The fourth time, my brother Albert laid his claim to the car. He had passed the driving test on the first try, right on his sixteenth birthday and insisted that he should get the car. After some consultation, my brother got what he wanted. I felt doubly devastated. Albert didn't go on that special ride in the car with my dad, the one where the magical engine sound lesson was revealed. It was clear to me that my father would have wanted me to inherit the Mustang. I was the one whose secret it had been shared with.

Albert still owns my father's Mustang today. The fact that it still has the original engine and grill gives him great pride. Whenever I go visit them, which is about every two or three months, I get to see it. The car that was supposed to be mine. Albert lives in the suburbs with his beautiful wife Gabriela and their son Watson whom we all call Wat. To be fair, Albert has taken good care of the car over the years. It's amazing that the thing still runs at all. I am not allowed to drive it. Not even for a spin around the block.

I know what you are thinking. I am a rational person. I realize that my father doesn't live inside that stupid old car. My father is alive in my memories and in my heart. Irrationally, I always felt that if I could own that car then somehow I could hold on to these memories a little bit more intensely.

I received back the most surprising email from Joshua. Instead of calling me the b word, he apologized, acknowledging how awkward our date had been. He told me he was coming out of a bad breakup and moving on has been painful for him. I can relate to that. He suggested we meet in a coffee shop for a quiet chat and promised to be on far better behavior. It is amazing how the human heart can flip from one side to the next in a split second like a windshield wiper. I was certain I never wanted to lay eyes on him

ever again. One little email and Bam! I am looking forwards to our coffee date.

If I am being honest, I don't know what drives me. What motivates me to go from point A to point B. Today during my lunch break I bought a paper map of San Francisco. Yes! I know that it's very hipster of me to get the old fashioned kind instead of looking it up on my laptop. Unfolding the map in my hands gave me a thrilling sensation. I resolved to study it like an ancient explorer with the aim to create a plan for my visit. I will be at the conference from 9-3 for five days, but I have the evenings and one weekend to fill with exciting adventure. Sam looked at my map and wrinkled her nose: "Woooooh! I haven't held one of those in ages. It feels so different looking at it this way." Cheryl appeared in the periphery. "Where did you get that? I can hardly believe they still sell maps these days."

"You will walk around San Fran holding up a map?" Asked Sam. "You will look like such a tourist."

"I know! I will be unique among all the other tourists. "I tried to laugh, but instead a snort came out. One of my not so attractive habits.

"So retro," said Cheryl, seemingly impressed

"Who will Chris yell at while you're gone?" asked Sam.

"We'll put a large doll into Car's seat, Chris will scream at her and won't notice the difference," said Cheryl, laughing.

"He will notice the difference when nobody tells him to sit down, relax and breathe," said Sam.

"I can volunteer to play nurse while Car is away," said Cheryl.

All three of us laughed. I placed the folded map on my desk next to my mouse. Glancing at it throughout the day gave me a jolt of pleasure. Incredible how a simple object can make your life seem 1000 times better. A map is designed to make the big unfathomable world fit into your hands. You play god looking down on streets and landmarks. So under control. All within reach. Everything understood.

Park

"YOU'RE EITHER LUCKY in parking or Lucky in love," said Stephanie at our morning's team meeting. We were in the boardroom waiting for Cheryl to join us. Construction had started in the North Western side of the parking lot of the industrial complex our company is housed in. Since then everybody had been complaining how difficult it was to find a parking spot. A big chunk of the parking lot is occupied by various materials and machinery required for the building. Since I haven't been lucky in love and I don't own a car, then I get to eat crow on both sides of the equation. Cheryl rushed in apologizing for the delay, using the parking situation as an excuse: "I had to circle the parking lot three times before I was able to snag an empty spot for myself. Can you believe it?" We all nodded our heads in sympathy.

As I exited the boardroom I noticed that my San Francisco map had been moved from its usual position. I ran all the way to my desk to grab my prized possession. I unfurled the folded paper and held it right in front of my face. Tiny little red x marks had been added on certain streets in the downtown area. Are these important tourist attractions? Are these restaurants I am meant to patronize? Who cares? Who marked my map?

"I saw Chris hunched over your desk this morning as I was rushing to the boardroom," said Cheryl. I folded up my map back into a neat rectangular stack and marched towards Chris's office like a soldier on a military parade. His door was ajar. I barged in without knocking and without asking for permission to enter. I was planning to start yelling but for some reason I noticed an odd-looking baseball cap on his head—a brown beanie looking thingy with a yellow silhouette of an elk or some other antlered animal. My distraction stopped me from yelling. Instead I said: "Hey! Nice cap." This was one of those situations where you want to say "Man, that is ugly!" but instead you say something nice. Why do I do that? I just couldn't get past how ugly that thing looked on top of his head. Chris smiled and fingered the rim of his cap with his right hand looking very pleased with himself: "My favorite team!" I wanted to say that it looked like he was wearing the poo emoji on his head, but instead I stayed silent, letting my revulsion pass. Finally I lifted the map to bring it into view. "Did you leave marks on my map?"

"I love San Francisco," he said. "Been there many times." He took the map out of my hand and unfolded it on his desk. Then his passed his fingers on the red x's he had marked about an hour ago.

"These are all the best spots to pick up prostitutes in San Francisco." His answer was so shocking I didn't know how to respond. Was he saying that I needed to know where to pickup prostitutes because he expects me to be a customer or a service provider? I didn't want to ask. Didn't want to find out what is behind his twisted thinking. I simply grabbed the map and marched out of his office, map flailing behind me like a cape. After that I felt disgusted each time I glanced at my map I had to throw it in the garbage. There goes my well manicured fantasy of San Francisco. Now I feel angry at myself. I should have ripped a layer off his face for what he did.

Sam said: "Essentially, he is calling you a whore."

Cheryl said: "I would have punched him in the face."

Bianca said: "You should have kept the map as evidence when making a sexual harassment complaint."

Judy said: "Who cares, you are going to San Francisco for a whole week. A stupid map can be replaced. Just ignore him."

My mother said: "Poor man. He must be very lonely. Try to be nice to him."

My second date with Joshua was a complete shock. It's like he became a different person over three days. Since last time I saw him, he had a hair cut. All the jewellery and piercings were gone. He was wearing a pressed cotton shirt and jeans. He looked sober. The

biggest shock was that he started the conversation by telling me about how his favorite brand of coffee comes from Uganda because the coffee beans are consumed by mountain goats then pooped out. Only then they are roasted and ground. I was stunned by the transformation but didn't comment on it. He was alert, attentive and even charming. Here is the best part—he is a car mechanic. I always wanted to marry a car mechanic. Even as a little girl. You can go ask my mother. Ever since I was eight, I always proclaimed to the world that my future husband would certainly be a mechanic. Who knows? Perhaps this is the one. Like the guy I am meant to spend the rest of my life with. I can visualize a future with this man. A house, two kids and sharing a car. I am for certain going to meet him again. So glad I didn't judge him by the first meeting. I can already visualize both of us telling the funny story of our first date— ours was love at second sight. The first sight was revulsion on both sides. Everybody at the party will laugh as we both make googly eyes at each other. Charming all around.

Stop

FOUR STOPS PAST my destination. That is the kind of day I am having today. First I got on a super crowded bus that smelled like a hot roast beef sandwich. I was hanging off the grab handle in my right hand, while trying to keep hold of my handbag with my left. This must be my best impression of a monkey yet. I was facing an oblivious seated young man cradling a tablet. He was reading the news. "Breaking News" The headlines screamed. "Saudi Arabia To Allow Women To Drive." I got irritated. Fuck them. Fuck their liberation. Fuck all Saudi women. It was comforting to know, that somewhere, out there, there was a magical land where I belonged. Where all women couldn't drive. The idea of being unable to drive was common, normal, even prescribed. An idea of a place where my defining feature was out of my hands. The fact that it's up to me is a

form of torment. I was so busy cursing Saudi women that I missed my bus stop and was forced to walk 9 blocks to get to work. But that is not even the worst part of my day. A far bigger calamity was ahead of me.

Every once in a while when I see a stop sign I hear the song: *Stop! In the name of love* in my head. I imagine Diana Ross and the Supremes materializing magically to convince cars and buses to obey the white on red sign.

Of all my friends, or more accurately, people I thought were my friends, Hakeem is the only one who stayed in touch with me after the divorce. He would call me every few weeks, we would have a coffee together and go for a walk along the beach. He looked like he was feeling sorry for me.

I was happy when he invited me to his wedding. He had travelled to Morocco, met a young woman his mother and sister chosen for him, and gotten married within two weeks. Now his bride had been shipped over to reside with her shiny new husband. There will be a second wedding celebration for all his local friends. Two days ago, he phoned me at home. He hummed and hawed. After stuttering for a few minutes, he told me that Ismail would be at the wedding with his new wife.

"I realize that this might be a little uncomfortable for you," he said.

"He got remarried?" I was in shock. "To whom?"

"To Fatin, about three months ago?"

"How did he meet her?" I was doing my best not to cry.

"It was an arranged marriage," Hakeem said.

"What a loser," I snorted.

"Please remember that I am having an arranged marriage as well," He said, sounding offended.

"O, yeah! Right! Sorry!" I can be so thoughtless sometimes.

"I would understand if you decided not come."

"No, no, no, I want to come," I said. "I am really looking forward to your wedding." Now it was my turn to sound conciliatory.

Fatin. Fatin. Fatin. Her name circled in my head like an accelerated car axle. So he left me for a woman he didn't know. An idea of a woman. A different woman. A hypothetical woman. This hurts like a son of a bitch. I wish he had met somebody. Fallen in love or in lust. And left me to pursue this other, better woman. Sexier woman. Younger woman. Prettier woman. More intelligent woman. More socially conscious woman. I could deal with that. I

could understand. Not this. He left me to leave me. Fuck Fatin and fuck Saudi women. Fuck all the hairy smelly women of Arabia.

Stop! In the name of love

I lay down on the carpet on my living room, legs and arms sprawled, and spent 3 or 4 hours staring at the curtain flailing in the gentle breeze coming from the half open window. Every little movement had a meaning. At first the fabric was oscillating in a simple back and forth movement. And then it was bulging out, billowing outwards in a pregnant shape before letting all the captured air escape. We bought these curtains together. We walked into one of those big-box stores. I couldn't decide on which curtains I liked, but Ismail liked these grey curtains that had a curvy loopy design on them. I wasn't convinced of his choice, but I went along with it. Once we hung them in our living room I was awestruck by how good they looked. The color and design complemented our existing furniture perfectly. I had no idea that Ismail was in touch with his inner Martha Stewart. I wonder if that is why he left me. He wanted to have children. We had discussed starting a family many times. Most recently had been two days before we bought these curtains. I had said that I wasn't ready yet. "Maybe in a year or two," I had said. Ismail had scratched his chin. Rested his head on the couch and said: "Alright then, I will wait for another year or two." For a split second he had had that look on his face. A forlorn expression. Had he told me it was urgent for him I would have been willing to get persuaded. The same way I changed my mind about which curtain to buy. I mean my opinion on babies wasn't set in stone. Why didn't I say "I can't wait to have your babies!" Maybe it

would have made him feel loved. I wonder if that is one thing that Fatin has that I don't. A ready baby happy attitude. A womb designed for production.

Before you break my heart

I pulled my arms together. Stopped staring at the curtain. Pushed myself up from the carpet. And decided that I would go to this wedding looking like the best vixen I could be. I would make Ismail regret ever leaving me.

But this time before you leave my arms
And rush off to her charms

I washed over the shores of the shopping mall like a mermaid desiring to become a human and swam out with a shopping bag containing a few select items that promised to turn me into a she-devil. Stop sign red dress with a lacy back and a flared out skirt. Elegant tan shoes. And a fuchsia hot lipstick to boot.

Baby, baby

I arrived at the wedding fashionably late by 30 minutes. A quick glance at the seating chart revealed that I was seated at the "efringa" table. The table for all the non-Moroccans. How times have changed. I used to feel so happy not to be seated on that table in the past. And here I am. I am lucky I am invited at all. I don't dare complain lest I don't get invited to future happenings.

But is her sweet expression

I glanced at Ismail across the room but pretended that I didn't notice him. My heart sunk as Fatin walked towards his table, pulled

back the chair and sat her skinny spindly body next to his. Was that a pregnancy bump? I think she's knocked up already! So this is it. This is the reason I got dumped. Not even beautiful. Younger yes, but not beautiful. Average looking with a scowl.

Worth more than my love and affection?

Jerk

MY BUS RIDE home today was crowded. I was sandwiched between a hairy Latin-looking young man and an Asian teenager who was wearing ear pods and thumbing at his cellphone nonstop. The bus came to a sudden stop. Everybody swayed in unison. And the hairy guy spilled his coffee on my shirt. "Thank god I am on my way home," was the first thought that came to my mind. Imagine if this happened first thing in the morning and I had to go through a whole day with a stain that looks like the continent of Africa on my right boob. "Sorry, sorry, I am so sorry!" the young man kept repeating. He even fished out a paper napkin from his back pocket and was about to start wiping the spill. But then he noticed the location of it and stopped. He handed me the napkin offering me a further apology.

Everybody knows that the smoothest ride is the one where you are cruising along at the same speed, there is no action on your speedometer when you move the same amount forward every second. You can also have smooth acceleration or deceleration, when your speed changes at the same rate over time. The speedometer climbs steadily. You are cruising down the road at a steady speed when a group of school children suddenly appear in front of you. You slam your foot on the brakes and the car jerks you out of your seat in the direction of the windshield. Smooth ride no more.

We had been walking on a sunny day in the downtown area. Ismael and I had just purchased matching sunglasses and walked down the road as if we were the coolest couple in the world. As if we were both Tom Cruise from the movie *Top Gun*. Swaggering about with foolish confidence. When in a moment of reckless abandon, I had turned to Ismail:

"Do you love me?"

"Of course I do," Ismail said, smiling back.

"How much do you love me?" I squeezed my right shoulder against his left for a hint of a snuggle.

"I would do anything and everything for you," Ismail said, reciprocating in a rare public display of affection by reaching over to hold my hand.

"Anything?" I asked.

"Anything." Ismail sounded certain. He even looked happy.

I looked across the street into the distance. I saw a topless man air boxing all by himself at the stairs of the Grand Art Gallery. Sweat was streaming down his bulging muscles as he proceeded to vanquish invisible enemies with his fists. A frenzied energy surrounded him. Everybody walking by was making an effort to avoid him. I pointed at the boxing man.

"Do you see that man over there? I want you to walk up to him and punch him right in the face." My right cheek was so close to his left cheek I could almost feel his stubble scratching me.

"Why would I do that?" Ismail said, letting go of my hand.

"Prove to me that you mean what you said."

"No," he said, backing away from me.

"You said you would do anything for me. I want you to prove it," I said. Here goes my logical side.

Ismail had let go the momentary bubble of bliss and walked away from me. A single quick motion of short duration. I guess that is the definition of the word jerk.

Makes me think of Antar returning after three years with the red camels only for Abla to make additional demands on him. Was I the unreasonable Abla in this scenario?

Enough with the drive down memory lane. Back to my present. I was meeting Judy and Bianca for drinks at a local pub. I was telling them about David, my driving instructor, who keeps referring to "your culture" as if I immigrated from a far away place, when Judy chimed in: "I am not surprised at all. You changed so much after you met Ismail."

"No I haven't! I am exactly the same person." I was expecting sympathy from my friends, not a critique.

Bianca nodded her head: "Once you started dating Ismail you adopted his body language. You even started speaking with an Arabic accent."

"But I don't even speak Arabic."

"Precisely! It was weird. Luckily the accent has waned since your separation," said Bianca.

"I refuse to believe that I have an accent when English is the only language that I speak," I said, scratching my head.

"Accent is only the tip of the weirdness. You became obsessed with learning how to cook Moroccan food. Since when was Car interested in cooking? Remember that dreadful lamb tagine you made for us?" Judy held her tummy as she laughed.

"You started taking belly dancing classes!" Now Bianca was laughing.

"Ismail actually disapproved of the dance classes, but I took them because they were fun."

"You started talking about social injustice and the effects of colonialism on third world nations," Bianca said, miming putting on reading glasses.

"That's an important subject," I said.

"You forgot all your friends," She said.

"The sooner you admit that you became weird once you met Ismail, the sooner you can put it all behind you," Judy said, waving a finger in my face.

"I guess love does strange things to people." I looked down at my feet.

The dreaded meeting with friends where I am the main project in progress was upon me. There was no escaping it. I keep waiting for the occasion when Judy is the focus of Bianca's and my expert advice on everything that is wrong in her life. There is no point in resisting. I might as well submit to the group desire and get it over with.

After going over the failure of my marriage we graduated to talking about who I should go out with. Judy volunteered to introduce me to a smorgasbord of eligible bachelors at a dinner party. Judy's husband, Andrew, is a high flying industrial designer and she thought at least three of his buddies would interest me. Bianca pitched in by suggesting that I meet some of her husband's co-workers. Emmerson is a car sales person and his chums fit the criteria of what would constitute the perfect boyfriend for me. Funnily enough neither one of them asked me what I was looking for in a potential boyfriend. As part of my heartbreak recovery I wrote down a detailed list of things I am looking for in a man. I read in an article on the internet that if you can visualize what you are looking for down to the most minute detail it increases the chances of it coming true.

Car's Wish List for a Future Boyfriend:

Sandy brown straight hair.

Doesn't wear socks to bed.

Not obsessed with books, average interest in novels is ok. One novel a month max. Less would be preferable.

Never read Dostoyevsky or Kafka.

Gainfully employed. No aspiring actors or artists.

Finds me genuinely interesting.

Is fantastic in bed. As in ravishes me and takes over and makes me feel tingly good afterwards.

Is not into anything kinky. S&M is not an option. Just plain good sex. Role playing is ok as long as it isn't anything too weird.

Loves to give foot massages.

Not impotent.

Doesn't take Viagra.

Knows how to please a woman in bed and takes interest in learning how to please me specifically.

Is an excellent driver. Knows how to parallel park, handle heavy traffic.

Offers to come pick me up on a date and drives me to the place.

Doesn't tell me stories.

Doesn't make fun of my lack of interest in reading.

Doesn't make fun of me at all, some teasing is ok.

Hates the opera Carmen and all operas in general.

Loves heavy metal but is not a musician himself.

Loves rap music, especially Eminem.

Takes genuine interest in what I have to say.

His name is not any variation of Ismail.

Is not a Moroccan, preferably not an Arab, although Iranians are ok.

Knows how to cook.

Would love to play Mario Kart with me for hours.

Is healthy and fit but not super athletic. No gym rats.

Enjoys normal food. Obsession with organic and health food is a turnoff.

Not a vegetarian.

Makes me laugh and finds my jokes funny.

Not so emotionally well-adjusted that I find him irritating.

Finds my work interesting.

Loves partying and going to concerts.

Doesn't talk about social justice. Not ever.

The world spirituality is not part of his vocabulary. Never says the word "journey".

Doesn't see a therapist.

Is not a therapist nor a psychiatrist.

Doesn't live with his mother.

Doesn't lecture me about post colonialism or orientalism.

Doesn't lecture me about anything.

Is easy to be around. I feel relaxed when I am with him.

Never says demeaning or abusive things to me.

Doesn't have a temper. Never punches holes in the wall and kick things when he is angry.

Doesn't want to travel the world, especially not India, is perfectly happy right here and now.

No chanting.

Wants to get married but doesn't talk about having children.

Smiles lots.

Tall and handsome.

Not a taxi driver, bus driver ok.

Has no desire to save the world.

Doesn't talk about becoming a better person.

Has no children from a previous relationship.

Doesn't talk about his ex all the time.

Is a maximum 4 years older or younger than me.

Enjoys dancing.

Thinks that I am unbelievably beautiful.

Takes time to gaze lovingly into my eyes.

Finds my dream of buying a pistachio green car charming.

Gets along with my family.

Buys me small thoughtful gifts to express his affection. Doesn't have to be anything expensive. CD, keychain or scarf are fine.

Enjoys fine dining.

Never wears tye-dye.

Is not curious about other cultures.

Speaks just English and has no desire to learn another language.

Easy going and flexible.

Thinks that *Maude and Barlow* is the best romantic movie in the world.

Enjoys going to the movies, action movies are ok.

Doesn't have to enjoy romantic comedies but is willing to come see them with me once in a while.

Walks and carries himself in a confident way.

Has a positive and optimistic outlook on life.

Must love the movie *Silence of the Lambs*.

Is not averse to having a discussion about zombies or vampires.

Is not a total gamer, some gaming time is acceptable.

Owns his own car.

Enjoys going for long drives in his car.

Is not obsessed with being environmentally friendly.

Not a smoker.

Enjoys being around other people. Relaxed in social situations.

Has many friends.

Gets along with my friends.

Will force me to get my driving licence and buy my own car.

Will not make fun of my job.

Knows how to dress and if not, is willing to take advice in that department.

Is not super stingy with money, doesn't feel guilty about spending it on fun stuff.

Likes to sleep in on the weekend.

Gets along with his family.

Doesn't hold grudges.

Doesn't behave as if the whole world is conspiring against him.

Loves pancakes and other breakfast food.

Appreciates fine cheese.

Hates olive oil and olives.

Skid Marks

THIS MORNING CHRIS came over and yelled at me for changing the name of the application in my documentation. I tried to explain to him that this was done at the behest of my boss and she was ordered to make that change by her boss, and so on. The marketing team had renamed Excalibur to the RemoteSenseTX project. No amount of reason could placate Chris. "This is my code! My application! You're stealing my work and deforming it! You have no right! You've ruined everything that I have spent the last two years working on!" After the ceremonial serving of a glass of water to get him to calm down, he said something that shocked me. "The only reason you are being sent to San Francisco is because management felt sorry for you. You have me to thank for that." I was more bothered by this than any obscenity he has yelled at me. It's

humiliating enough to be putting up with his abuse. It's a whole other thing to be receiving payment for it, likes a prostitute. So that's what the red x marks referred to. Well done Chris. Insult expertly delivered. Antar himself would have felt hurt.

This reminded me of the story that Ismail made up on one of my sleepless nights. An Ismail classic. He told me this story while softly smoothing by hair back. There was such affection in our marriage.

Da Falihi Can

I finally read The Da Vinci Code. It is a well written and a suspenseful piece of garbage. I suspect Dan Brown has Arabic ancestry—for only a mind baked by the desert sun would cook up a hodgepodge of art, religion, murder and history and conspiracy theories. And then forgo logic and declare proudly: "Ta-da! I present to you a novel." I wonder what would it be like, if The Da Vinci Code was written by an Arab untainted by western influence. My guess is it wouldn't be well written. It would pretend to be suspenseful yet lack suspense the way beauty pageants lack the essence of beauty. Given our fondness for drama, treachery disguised as nobility would pop up in every nook and cranny of the story. The plot would be a derailed train, but it would be amusing. Much more amusing than the western version. So here is my Arabic version of The Da Vinci Code. Check your brain at the door and prepare to be bamboozled.

Imagine an ancient secret society of weirdoes meeting in an underground hall somewhere in the US. These are a group of

frustrated middle age men and a few women obsessed with taking nude pictures of unsuspecting victims. Meetings like this have been taking place for four thousand years. Traditions and ceremonies have been refined to an ultimate perfection. Each meeting has an imposing presence, the way a fat lady singing at the opera commands attention across all ages.

They perform secret handshakes, then recite their motto, which they all have memorized by heart. Their mission? To Photograph The Unwilling Undressed. At last they get to sit around a candlelit oak table. They move on to the next item on their agenda—modern difficulties with taking nude pictures of disinclined people. In the good old days, the Secret Society of Weirdoes (SSW) worried about social ostracization and legal prosecution for pursuing their God-given obsession. However, in more recent days, a new set of problems are challenging this proud group. It's becoming increasingly difficult to take nude pictures of people who do not want to be pictured in the nude. For one thing, the number of people refusing to expose themselves is sharply declining in America. As we see in home movies and American college videos, American people will gladly take off their clothes for a glass of beer, for a smile or even to get five seconds of mere passing attention. Big celebrities are leaking their own sex videos on purpose to increase their fame. For the SSW, taking pictures with cooperating subjects is a no-no. It's just no fun if the subject is willing. Secondly, figures of authority are no longer above reproach. In the past priests, police officers and politicians were above scrutiny. When pictures were taken of those people, the shock value provided months' worth of satisfaction for

SSW members. But in today's sad and skeptical society people look with suspicion even upon the clergy. People expect priests to be child molesters, politicians to have illicit affairs with interns and police officers to be cavorting with drug dealers and prostitutes. The novelty of such discoveries is all but worn out. SSW members shake their heads at their sad state worrying that their ancient society will become extinct. This is when Freddy, the bright one in the group, came up with a plan. He said something like this.

"Let's create a powerful lobby group that pretends to embody good Christian values. We will use our influence to put an unsuspecting poor soul into the White House. Then we convince this God-fearing poor soul to invade a country because it has non-existing weapon of mass destruction. Proudly, this new president will declare to the nation; "We need to liberate that country and give them democracy". Then we infiltrate those silly left wing groups and whisper in their ears that it is all for oil, so that all sides will be confused about the real motivation. We must select a conservative country with a very modest population. A country where people never show up nude, not even in front of their own families. A country where women are covered up from head to toe and men are covered up from neck to toe. For example, Iraq. Then when the war starts, we all will volunteer as soldiers, claiming patriotic feelings. We make sure not to fight and keep our heads low and volunteer to guard the prisoners. And once in place, we go wild, take nude pictures of modest Iraqis of all shapes and sorts. Then we will create a scandal and those pictures will be published in every newspaper and TV station so that our comrades back home can

enjoy them as well. I predict that even the most respectable of news agencies won't be able resist publishing those pictures when they have their hands on them. We might even get new recruits into the SSW! Looking at nude pictures of Iraqis will become the new American past time. We will gain a new legitimacy that we never had before. We will be able to take all the nude pictures we want. Heck! I even predict that we will be able to get nude pictures of the Iraqi president ..... that man they call Saddam. They call us perverts now but they will start calling us heroes once all our countrymen are swept up in our favorite pastime."

Everybody in the room looked unconvinced. "But that is is too complex and elaborate," said Billy Bob "I can't believe that a mainstream news agency like CNN would broadcast nude images of Iraqis against their wishes .... I just can't see it happening," said Jeremiah. "You think we can fool all those intellectual leftwing people to believe that it's all for oil?" said Hilary.

Freddy pounded the table with his fists. "Unless one of you is able to come up with a better plan I suggest we stick to mine. These are desperate times and we need desperate actions."

Who knew that the wacky plan would work so well? The Weirdoes Society was very pleased with the progress achieved in a short time.

The whole Middle East was plunging into despair and humiliation. Nude pictures of Iraqis were popping up in mainstream media on a daily basis. The shame was destroying the spirit of this once modest nation. Nobody was safe. Everybody knew it would be

their turn next to have their picture taken. A whole nation prepared to live out the rest of its life in shame.

That is when our hero Falah comes in. A historian and a scientist, Falah comes across a set of secret documents that reveals to him the existence of the Weirdoes Society. He then walks around the Louvre in Paris and sees all the paintings of nude people done by all the great masters. Da Vinci, Rafael, Michelangelo—they were all obsessed with staring at nude bodies. Falah puts two and two together and figures out that the war was not about oil, nor about weapons nor about democracy, it was about our nude assess. He tries to expose the conspiracy, but nobody believes him.

The director of the United Nations, Slofi Banan, tells him that since the gravy train of food for oil program ended he has had to live off of his meager UN salary and has no time to think about elaborate conspiracies.

The director of the CIA assures him that the American public is not interested in hairy Iraqi ass.

The director of Al Jazzeera refuses to air the story because talking about ass and nudity goes against their moral code.

In despair, Falah returns to Iraq knowing that he has to take matters into his own hands. He works day and night in a laboratory custom built in the basement of his house until he discovers Falihi spray. Falihi spray is a substance distilled from sand. When applied to human skin produces ultra violet light undetectable to the human eye yet deadly to camera lenses. It jams all cameras, regardless of their kind. In place of a nude body the picture appears with a black blob instead. Falah travels all across Iraq disguised as a holy man,

telling people that the Falihi spray is a holy substance blessed by religious clerics. All the people start applying the Falihi spray and all nude pictures of Iraqis appear with big black blobs. The SSW members start withdrawing from the army because their plan has failed.

A group of Islamic terrorists discover the true nature of the Falihi spray and steal huge quantities of it. They travel to the US and apply the spray on American actresses, fashion models and porno stars. This causes a complete collapse of American pop culture, and Hollywood producers vow to make movies in accordance to Islamic shari'a laws, to avoid penalization of their top talent and the destruction of all their camera equipment

Falah becomes a popular figure and is voted to be the next Iraqi president. During his inauguration he announces his love to Fahima (whom I forgot to introduce earlier in the story in order to make this more of a compelling ending). Fahima accepts his marriage proposal. Fahima and Falah get married in a big ceremony in the middle of Fardous square and there is dancing and singing all night long. Their wedding photo is one big happy black blob.

Both American and Iraqi people live happily ever after and the members of the Weirdoes society go to therapy to help them heal from their evil ways.

The End.

At the time I thought that Da Falihi Can demonstrated that Ismail had a wild imagination. Now I can see how much he despised Western culture. I wonder if he saw me as a member of the Secret Society of Weirdoes.

Earlier in the day, Stephanie sauntered forth to let us know that the CTO of our company was planning a visit to our office in two days. This is the highest top executive from the corporate head office, coming to visit us. The purpose of his visit was to see a demo of RemoteSenseTX and to get a status update about deployment plans to our first customer.

"I don't think he will want to meet with any of you, but just in case, let's all be on our best behavior on that day," said Stephanie.

To that Cheryl immediately replied: "Let's hope the milk thief doesn't strike on that day. It would be embarrassing if the CTO takes his coffee with milk and we only have whitener to offer him."

"There will be no talk of milk thief or anything else negative on that day. Just stay sharp and positive," Stephanie snapped. It was rare to see her like that. She is usually the essence of patience.

Assembly Line

AFTER MY DATE with Joshua I rushed home to finish up work before my trip. I was editing the reference manuals, changing all the names of the application from Excalibur to RemoteSenseTX. You might be right to think that would be a simple word replace function. However there are hundreds and hundreds and thousands of screen shots with the application name prominently displayed. I told Stephanie that we should wait with the work because I have a feeling that soon they will change the logo and it will mean redoing all the work again. But I was shut down. It was 10:30 before I managed to go to sleep. The next day, I got up bright and early and called a taxi to get me to the airport.

I was waiting outside when my purple chariot arrived. I had my brown suitcase sitting next to my feet, rubbing against my calves

like a cherished pet and the handbag that Sylvester gave me hanging off my shoulder. The taxi driver jumped out of his car with enthusiasm. He swept my luggage from underneath me with a circular arm movement. As soon as he lifted it off the ground he grunted: "Aaaaaaa! It is so heavy! Why do women always have heavy luggage?" I didn't say anything. But I wanted to say: "I didn't ask you to carry my suitcase, you volunteered to do it, so quit complaining." Instead I quietly sat in the back seat where I saw that I was being driven by Rajiv.

"Are you Mexican?" Rajiv asked.

Oh no! Another taxi driver who wants to have a conversation. I wish I could roll my eyes, but Rajiv was looking at me through the rearview mirror so I had to restrain myself.

"No!" You would think that would be the end of it.

"Are you sure?"

"Yes," I said, after a sigh.

"Really? When I saw you from a distance I was certain that you were Mexican." Rajiv tilted his head up.

"Hmmmm! That's interesting." Our eyes met in the rearview mirror.

I said that last thing hoping it would end our inane exchange.

"So where are you from?" He had to look away to pay attention to oncoming traffic.

I had failed in my mission to sit in the backseat in silence.

"I am from here." I looked out the window.

"No I mean where are you from originally? I am from India myself," he said with a happy lilt in his voice.

"I am from here, born and raised." I leaned my head against the window.

"Nah! you are not." He lifted his right hand off the steering wheel and pointed his palm out. The same way you see a buddha statue sometimes.

I said nothing.

"You are from Mexico, you just want to hide it."

A bright red car passed us in the other direction. I noticed that the driver was picking his nose. People forget that they are still in public when they are in their car.

"Most people who have accents don't hear other people's accents, but I am different," he said. "I can hear your accent. You think I can't but I do."

"I have no accent." I paused between each word for emphasis.

"You are not fooling me, I am certain English is not your first language. You are like me, but you don't want to admit it." He made a clicking sound with his tongue.

"English is my only language, I'm afraid." The situation moved from being annoying to being ridiculous.

"Are you sure you don't speak Spanish?" He combed his hair back with the palm of his hand.

"Yes, I am certain I don't speak Spanish." I snorted.

How many times do I have to say the same thing before I am believed?

"But you look so foreign. It is not just your accent. Even your body language says I am not from here. I could tell from the way

you were standing by the curb," he said, throwing me another glance in his rear-view mirror.

"Mmm."

What I really wanted to say is: "I don't care, just shut up and drive me to the airport."

"The way you had your arms around yourself as if you were bracing yourself. The way you didn't look me in the eye when I spoke to you and instead looked on the ground. The way you were standing on one leg, letting your body symmetry sag in one direction. I notice all these things. Everything about you says I don't belong here." Both his hands were gripping the steering wheel as as he slammed on the brakes to stop for a red light.

"Oh yeah?" I said as I was getting jerked out of my seat.

"Yeah, yeah, yeah. Us taxi drivers, we notice everything. We are better than Sherlock Holmes. You know who Sherlock Holmes is? Right? My job is to assess a client from one glance. With one look I can tell who is crazy, who is drunk, who is trouble, who has no money and who is in trouble. That way I can figure out who not to let into my taxi. But I can also tell much much more. I can tell you things about yourself that you don't want to know. I can tell you things about yourself that if I told you, you would think I was psychic. But I am not psychic, I am just very good at assessing people from one glance."

"Are you ever wrong?" I asked.

"I am never wrong. I am telling you I got the magic taxi driver abilities." He was tapping his right index finger on the steering

wheel as he took a sharp right. My body tilted to the left, pressing against the car door.

"Well you are wrong about me. You will never be able to say that again."

Silence.

Thank God! I think I finally shut him up.

"What is your name?" He said while a police car drove past us making a wee woo siren sound.

"Car," I said.

"What nationality is that?" Rajiv's eyes were following the police car.

"It has no nationality, it's just a name."

"Every name has a nationality," Rajiv said, and clicked his tongue.

"My name is an exception to that rule."

Awkward silence swirled in the air between us. I wished I could say to him: "If you are such a Sherlock Holmes, then you would be able to figure out that I want to be left alone. I don't want to tell you my life story. Where I come from is none of your business. I told you the truth in every answer I gave you. I don't want to hear what you have to say about me. The things you gleaned about my personality are all wrong. All your assessments of people perhaps give you comfort or make you feel safe. I guess your job is sometimes dangerous. I guess you need to tell yourself a bunch of crap to give yourself the sense that you are in control. That you will sniff out the serial killer and prevent him from getting into your car. I guess your pretend detective abilities allow you to get out of the

house in the morning and do this crappy job so you can send money to your extended family back in India. But you are wrong. You are lying to yourself. Your whole fantasy is a scrap heap. I can explain this to you but it might break your heart. It might paralyze you. Cost you your livelihood. Hurt your family. I guess you need to entertain yourself in this boring job you do. If you tell yourself that you can psychoanalyze your clients then you can walk around pretending you are doing some good in this world. Your clients are also your patients. You are not a taxi driver, you are a therapist. Your job serves a higher purpose. But that is a falsehood. You are just a driver. You get people from location a to location b. No magic. No Story. Something banal. Simple. Boring even. One day a machine will do your job. Your whole life is boring and meaningless. And most importantly, the one thing I want to say to you with ardent passion is that: I have NOTHING to say to you. Nothing at all. Nada. Wala Ishi. Nic. Kloom. Zip. Not even a sound click. Not even a hand gesture. The nothingness that I have to express to you is so giant it would populate a whole stadium. The nothingness that exists between us sucks the air and creates a pocket of vacuum that prevents light from travelling. One million light years are not enough to bridge this gap. There is nothing worth saying this moment. Just drive and shut up!"

Help me lord! I still had another taxi driver to deal with at the other end before I got to my hotel.

/———//———//———/

The view from the airplane was glorious. From above San Francisco looks big and sparkly. Like a big alien mother ship beckoning its strayed citizens to come back from the far corners of the galaxy. A big calm descended upon my heart as the airplane approached the runway.

In San Francisco I was driven By Rahul, another fine gentleman from India. His opening question to me was, I kid you not, this: "Are you married?"

"No!" I said while listening to the tick tick tick sound his blinker made. How I love that rhythm.

"I am looking for a wife," he said, holding his hands on the steering wheel in the correct 9 and 3 position.

"Oh." I looked out the window to admire the grandiose highway that led to the city.

"Well! Clearly you are not interested, but maybe you know single women who are."

"Women?! How many wives are you looking for?" I asked.

"Come on! Surely you know some single women." He titled his head backwards.

"Yes I do." I nodded mine.

"Why not match them up with a nice man such as myself."

"Well, you live in a different city, for one."

"I am willing to move. For a good woman I would leave this awful city." He moved his right hand as if he was sweeping invisible dust off his dash board.

"Awful city?"

"The surface is all shiny but underneath it's all garbage," he said.

"What do you mean?"

"Everybody pretends they are liberal. However, you wouldn't believe the amount of racism that I face." His turned the right blinker on to take an exit. That glorious tick tick tick sound played again.

"I'm sorry to hear that," I said.

"You can help me out. Just give me the contact information of one of your nice friends and I would have the motivation to move away from this place."

Silence.

"Come on! I just know you have a nice lady on your mind right now. You can make two people happy with a simple introduction." We stopped at a red light smoothly. The busy downtown pedestrian traffic enveloped the car.

I didn't have a woman in mind but now that he mentioned it, the image of Sam popped in my mind. But what am I supposed to say to her? I gave your contact information to a random man I don't know at all?

"Sorry, but I can't help you," I said after a pause.

The rest of the ride he was sulking, but at least it was quiet in the car.

Seat Belt

TODAY I MET SYLVESTER on the bus. It's always a good day when I encounter Sylvester. He is one of those old-fashioned gentlemen that give me hope goodness still exists in the world. I love the way he actually listens to me, not just waits for his turn to speak. He pauses after I say something and responds after only sufficient pondering has taken place. I thanked him for the handbag and made sure to mention how useful it had been on my San Francisco trip. He nodded his head, smiled and asked me how I was doing. It was the quality of his presence, the kindness in his eyes that propelled me to answer truthfully.

As it happens, I am going through a period of massive sadness. In the past, I've heard people speak of being depressed, drowning in a sea of darkness, but I never comprehended what that was like. To

TAKE THE HIGHWAY

have no choice in the matter. To be thrown into a deep well that you can't climb out of. I used to believe sadness to be the contemplation of dark thoughts that lasted a few minutes or hours. I imagined that the afflicted were occupied, like myself, with the productive monotony of life the rest of the time. What I hate the most about my current state is how the past is pressing itself into my present. Incessantly. Obsessively. Every moment of every waking hour I find my thoughts picking over things said or done. Fragments of memory that are relived in a loop until all angles have been examined. It's like I am in a time warp and things happening right in front of my eyes are of less importance.

I would describe myself as a happy person, a cheerful person, an optimistic person. I didn't realize that I was just lucky. When my lucky toy car shattered into tiny little shards, I found myself befuddled by the unfamiliar territory. I have no choice but to move into a different sort of life. I feel like a foreigner visiting a strange country called my life. The streets and faces feel familiar, it's the quality of my looking that is rendering them peculiar.

In between sight seeing and attending keynote speeches in San Francisco, I had suddenly realized that I was experiencing a state of extreme unexpected euphoria. Once back, when I described my feelings during the trip to my friend Bianca, she was certain that either alcohol, drugs or sex was the culprit behind the mystery. When I assured her that none were present on the stage of reality, she didn't believe me. This experience was a bit of a mystery to myself as well. Here I was, all by myself, in a new city where I didn't know anybody, taking workshops that went over my head. I should

148

have felt lonely, alienated, frustrated with my limited abilities. To top it off, it rained and San Francisco was having unusually cold weather. The hotel room didn't have adequate heating and the electricity went out several times. The most irritating taxi rides. Ever. Things were breaking left, right and center. Cold showers, cold rain and a washing machine that was eating my clothes didn't put a dent in my mood. I did have moments of loneliness, feelings of yearning for my nephew especially. I did have moments of frustration and alienation. But overall, I was overwhelmed with elation—I felt like I was walking on clouds. When it rained, I wore my grey jacket, put on my hat, stuck my hands in my pockets and went outside singing "I am walking in the rain" to the tune of "I am singing in the rain". When the electricity went out in the hotel, I purchased candles and admired how romantic my tiny room felt. When the washing machine ate my t-shirts, I simply threw them out and purchased a cheap batch of new ones. I would be lying if I told you that I found a positive spin on taking cold showers when the water heater broke, but even that didn't put a dent in my mood. This puzzle has been nagging me in the back of my mind for a long time. Now that the divorced me had plenty of time, and with my happiness shattered to smithereens, I decided it would be helpful to sit down and reflect on what had happened and research my trip for clues that might help me build a new happiness chip to place inside my brain.

Clue Number One: the dummy factor. I was constantly lost all the time; I was the dummy that didn't understand what was going on around me. Unfamiliar streets. Strange city.

Clue Number Two: observer effect. When you are in a new city, you get to witness all sorts of things, but you have no way of assessing them. For example, I accidentally walked down an alley with a red brick wall. On this vast wall there was a sign for a free peep show. Nothing but that sign, a peep hole next to it and the long red wall. I looked through the eye piece to see what looked like a Victorian era pornographic short movie. It was interesting to watch, even intriguing. But as an outsider I have no clue as to the significance of this thing that I saw. Is this a San Francisco thing? The city is littered with these secret peep shows? Who runs this thing? And why? Things that might disturb me or bug me on more familiar turf, were simply observed with curiosity and not judged. Another thing that I noticed in my wandering about were curious red brick circles laid down in various street intersections. What was their purpose? Clearly they were not roundabouts. Were they ornamental? Is it a superstitious custom? Perhaps it is some kind of a joke, or maybe a common friendly gesture that is not to be taken seriously. In a new city, there is a moral ambiguity because there is no frame of reference to judge things by.

Clue Number Three: novelty of ordinary things effect. While in San Francisco my cappuccino tasted good each and every day. The ride on the cable car seemed like an adventure. I would wander around the city and feel mesmerized by every building I passed. A simple toast with jam in a coffee shop tasted like a prized treat. Even the graffiti on the walls of the grittier parts seemed interesting, and I don't like graffiti. I would eavesdrop on the conversations of people around me and enjoy getting an insight into their lives. The novelty

of everything leads to greater enjoyment of simple activities. Buying a yogurt at the corner store turns into an adventure.

Clue Number Four: Walking effect. On most days I walked for hours.

After contemplating my experiences in San Francisco I came up with a few additional items to add to my heal-my-broken-heart-project plan. I would pretend I was a foreigner in my own city, experiencing everything for the first time, suspending judgement about it. I would go for long walks and make an effort to admire beauty wherever I saw it. My last ingredient was a nightly visualization that I came up with. Every night, before going to sleep, I would visualize my heart as a dark box. Then I would visualize that a ray of light was coming through and over time filling the dark void. I would go to sleep imagining that the light was spreading throughout my body. All of this I told Slyvester, when he asked me how I was doing.

When I finished talking, Sylvester was looking at me intensely. I could tell from his body language that he was processing what I had told him. I appreciated that he didn't feel the need to tell me what to do or say something stupid like: "Time heals all wounds" or "Don't worry, you will get over it." Or some other meaningless inspirational quote that stupid people like to share on Twitter.

Instead he inhaled deeply and closed his eyes. After a while he said:

"I knew I saw a sadness in your eyes the very first time I met you. I don't have any words of wisdom to impart despite my old age. The older I get, the less I feel that I know. Young men can be over

confident and arrogant. I was certainly that way. I was married to the most fantastic woman in the world. She was smart, much smarter than me. Beautiful, elegant, dedicated mother and a true intellectual. Margery was the most fine person I ever had the pleasure to know. And yet through out my life I taken her for granted. I have no idea why she put up with me. My biggest regret in my life is the fact that I didn't make more effort to listen to her. She was the love of my life. I didn't appreciate that until after she was gone."

His response hit me right in the heart. I had no words. My eyes teared up. I wiped the edges with a paper napkin. We sat bobbing side to side in companionable silence as the bus ambled along in the busy morning traffic. Cars swished by spraying the side of the bus. Commuters got on and off. I felt engulfed in an organized flow of humanity. It was comforting.

At the office there was a great hush in anticipation of the CTO's visit. You could hear nothing but the hundreds of keyboards clicking. Sam poked her head out and whispered: "Guess what?" "What?" "The milk thief struck today of all days. The office manager had to run out to buy a fresh batch of milk." Cheryl then popped her head above the divider and whispered: "I heard he is coming at ten. I wonder what he looks like?" Sam whispered: "Probably a

nondescript white male." I nodded my head in agreement. All three did this mock silent laugh that is adorable as it's theatrical. The two disembodied heads slid down out of the view. I was grateful that I would have at least one day in the office without Chris yelling obscenities at me.

At about 10:30 all the keyboard clicking sounds stopped. A wave of silence splashed across the office. I discreetly lifted myself up ever so slightly by pushing my hands up on the desk yet keeping my legs contorted in a seated position, swiveling my head back to catch a peek. From a distance I would look as if I was seated on a tall chair. I felt very clever at my unique maneuver. I could see the CTO walking down the hallway with the R&D manager to his right, the Customer Service manager to his left, the Q&A manager right behind him, the office manager and Stephanie trailing behind them. Sam was right. The perfect nondescript white male. One glimpse was enough to satisfy my curiosity. A second would have been redundant. Five minutes later a wave of keyboard clicking washed over the office again. With all that peace and quiet I had a productive day. It's amazing how much work I can get done when nobody is screaming at me.

Around noon, I headed to the lunch room. I was heating up yesterday's lemon chicken and fried rice in the microwave when the CTO walked in. Yes! Mr. Big Wig himself. He was on his own. The entourage that had trailed him all day was nowhere to be seen. I felt awkward and didn't know how to behave. So I stared at the microwave's timer counting down the seconds as if I was witnessing a rocket being launched into outer space. 39. 38. 37. In my head I

was thinking: "This guy is my bosses' bosses' boss. If he was any more powerful he would be the big guy in the sky."

He introduced himself. "John Zielinski," he said, extending his right hand. I took it and shook.

"What do you do at the company?" He asked with a friendly smile.

"I am a technical writer," I said. The microwave started beeping but I ignored it.

"Now that I know what you do during the week, tell me about what you did last weekend."

"I volunteered at the homeless shelter serving dinner," I said. I don't know why I lied to him. I haven't done any volunteering since Ismail left me. Spending Sunday preparing and serving a meal at the Goodwill Center was something we did together once a month. I enjoyed the look of admiration I got from Ismail on those days. I would be in the industrial kitchen chopping leeks at the stainless steel counter wearing a handkerchief over my head for sanitary reasons, and I would look up and catch Ismail's gaze. It made me feel like Elizabeth Taylor in the movie Cleopatra. I think I wanted to say something to the CTO that would impress him. Instead he scrunched up his face and said:

"I don't understand why a successful woman such as yourself would choose to spend her spare time with losers."

This is exactly the type of person that Ismail despised. I could hear Ismail's voice whisper in my ear: "I can't believe that a good person such as yourself would work hard five days a week to make an

arrogant self righteous capitalist pig like him even richer than he already is so that he could become even more arrogant."

I smiled uncomfortably and said nothing. Serves me right for lying. If I had told him the truth by saying I had spent Sunday on my couch eating chips and watching meaningless youTube videos such as "top 10 car chases in movies" on my my laptop, maybe I would have impressed him more.

Later in the day my mother came over to my apartment and we ate dinner.

"I need to know what happened," she said between mouthfuls of tomato soup." Why did you get a divorce? You have been avoiding the subject for months. The time has come to discuss it."

"That's the thing. I don't know what happened. I thought I would be able to figure it out after few months. But I still don't know why Ismail left me." I placed my spoon down and stared out the window. A crane had been erected a few blocks away. I could see the tip of it out the window. Staring at that crane was comforting. Something new was being built somewhere not too far from me. I am not a complete curse on my surroundings.

"You are the equivalent of three men put together, I am not worried about you," said my mother, addressing my silent sadness. "The way you tackle everything, you roll up your sleeves and dive

into the thick of it. Ever since you were a little girl, you were fearless. I remember, one time, when you could barely walk. We went for a walk downtown. Among the busy traffic and hordes of pedestrians, you refused to hold my hand. You kept pulling away insisting on navigating this challenge on your own. To punish you, I hid in a side alley. My plan was to scare you by making you think that you got lost so that you would be happy holding my hand afterwards. As I looked at you from the side, you looked terrified. You turned around. You placed your hands in your pockets and kept walking forward. You didn't cry. You didn't call my name. You just kept walking straight ahead as if everything was fine. Albert, your brother, was a clingy child. Complete opposite from you. Always demanding to hold my hand. It felt as if he was attached to my hip. Look at him now. A father himself."

It's hard thinking of myself as a pillar of strength. At this point I feel like a debris floating in the wind. A meek person who doesn't stick her neck out for anyone, not even herself. I stick firmly within my lane without any need for a hand or turn signal. Of course I'm not a complete wreck. I am still rolling down the highway. And yet, everything might fall apart at any second.

"I don't know why Ismail left," my mother continued, "but there was always friction between the two of you. He always seemed out of place. You were turning yourself inside out to make him happy. What can I tell you? We women are stupid. We will do anything and everything to make the man in our life happy. Sometimes you can love somebody with all your heart and all your soul and still, it's not enough." She reached over to touch my hand.

"I am surprised to hear you talk like that. You were married to dad." I sighed.

"Your dad was a great dad, but he wasn't a perfect husband. Now is not the time to discuss that though," my mother said, withdrawing her hand and going back to eating soup.

"Since we are having a heart to heart," I said, "this is a good time to tell you. I hated the Opera Carmen." I stared at my mother's face to see the reaction.

My mother smiled: "I know."

Here we are. A widow and a divorcee talking about men, love and heartbreak. You will never see this in a movie or read about it in a novel because it's so pathetic it would kill any suspense in its tracks.

I stared at the crane out my kitchen window. All I could think of was the word "Despite". Despite the fact that I am a woman, despite my hair color, despite my circumstance, despite other people's expectations of me, despite of what the world might think, despite my short comings, despite is the declarative word of the English language. It announces itself like an elephant in a room, you might choose to ignore it, but it will force itself into your attention span whether you like it or not. Despite, is the samurai sword you carry in your scabbard ready to unleash at a moments notice. If you remove the d and e from despite it becomes spite, a word that reminds me of a fantastic Kathy Bates movie called *Delores Claiborne*. Despite leads you into victory, up the mountain, all the way to the top. Enough is never enough, there is always more to be

had. Despite is the reverse side of defeat. Today I am fragile despite my strength.

"You are right. I am strong. but I am sick and tired of being strong. I am now on a new mission to explore my fragile side," I said to my mom before picking up my spoon to eat.

Traffic Light

WATCH IT SWAY in the wind. The three-eyed gargoyle hanging from a wire looking down on you. Or perhaps more eerily still, perched on a pole. Winking in an infinite looping sequence—green yellow red green yellow red. Seen but unconsidered, passed under a dozen times a day by most of us, telling us when to move, shaping the rhythm of our lives, delaying our travel plans, and occasionally, inadvertently, playing a part in how we die or how we kill each other. Consider the humble traffic light.

I counted 32 traffic lights on my way to this Thanksgiving dinner before I stopped counting. I was trying to stay focused and pay attention. The man standing next to me bumped into me, I had to shuffle over to create some distance between us. Several traffic lights passed that I didn't count. After that I lost my motivation. It

159

took me three buses, two hours and utilizing the services of over 32 three-eyed gargoyles to get here. Our family is gathering at my brother's house. Ever since Watson was born, Albert has been hosting the family dinners. Or I should say Gabriela, his wife, is hosting us, since she is the one doing most of the work. Albert looks so grown up sitting at the head of the dining table. He is the definition of self possession. In his house. His wife beaming a smile at him as she brings in the turkey. His beautiful son getting loving attention from his grandmother. This lovely house. My father's Mustang parked in his garage. Here I am. Sitting with an empty chair to my right. The chair where Ismail sat, last year, at this very exact dinner table. I remember how I reached down under the table to hold Ismail's hand to reassure him the very first time he sat in that chair seven years ago. He was uncharacteristically nervous. I can still feel his rough calloused hand in mine.

Green yellow red green yellow red. Is there anything lonelier than a traffic light blinking to an empty road? It's an establishing shot in movies that screams: desolation. It plugs into our fear that the electronic world doesn't care about us, and will exist long after we're gone. The traffic light doesn't need people. It is perfectly happy doing its thing with or without our attention. And yet here's the thing: traffic lights don't really do anything. They can't physically stop you. They don't engage a barrier to prevent cars from going through the intersection. They don't raise that barrier when it's time to drive. They won't stop you from plowing into a hapless pedestrian at the intersection. No, they're only a prop, a signifier of a

social contract we've agreed to. They are a means of behavior change. We mostly obey.

Half way through dinner, Watson said: "Dad! Tell me a story about grandma's bad driving."

My mother, Ester, is a notoriously bad driver. Her driving foibles have reached such epic proportions that they have turned into family folk tales that will, no doubt, get handed down for many generations to come. Whenever we start telling stories of her bad driving, my mother shrugs it off. Participating with a laugh or two at her own expense.

And so Albert told a story.

"Your grandmother is such a bad driver, that one time she tried to park her red hatchback in the garage of the apartment building we lived in when I was a child. But instead she hit a column. She backed away and then moved forwards to hit the same exact column again. In the exact same spot. Backed away and did the same thing about four or five times before our neighbour Mr. Reid rescued her by volunteering to park the car for her."

Watson was cradling his face in mock surprise. Delighted to the max with the story. The rest of us laughed heartily.

I chimed in, waving a hand at Albert to get his attention.

"Remember the time mom got lost driving home from the mall? She stopped the car in the middle of the road to have a cry. A policeman stopped his car to ask her what was wrong. When she explained to him that she didn't know how to get home, he volunteered to drive ahead so that she could drive behind him all the way back home. For months people in the neighborhood talked

about how our mom came home escorted by the police. Nobody believed that it was a simple case of getting lost."

More laughter erupted in the dining room.

Before I had the chance to finish my story and bask in the glory of the laughter afterwards, Albert rushed in:

"Or that time Mum bought 25 burger buns from the bakery. She placed all the groceries in the trunk, but left the bag with the bread on the roof of her car. Other drivers kept honking at us while bread flew in the air in a random formation. Mom kept complaining: 'Why is everybody so grumpy today?' She only realized what was going on once we arrived home. Only three burger buns were left."

At this point Watson was rocking forwards and backwards, clutching his stomach with the force of his laughter. Gabriel tried to stop us: "Come on guys. This sounds like a bunch of exaggerations."

"O o o" I protested that last statement by spreading the palms of both of my hands across the table.

I marvel at the genius of the yellow light. The yellow light creates an ephemeral zone of decision around the intersection. When a light turns yellow, approaching drivers have a choice to make, in a split second: do I speed up and drive through the yellow light, or do I slow down and stop? David, like all driving instructors will of course always tell you that a yellow light means slow down and prepare to stop, but on the street, that's not always how it works. Sometimes it really would be more dangerous to stop than to run the yellow. And sometimes those driving instructors like David

are right: running the yellow is a terrible, dangerous idea. How do you know which is which?

Yellow lights generally last three to five seconds. Which means when one appears, in the space of about a second, you've got to do a few intense calculations: how far you are away from the intersection, how fast you're going, how clear the intersection is, and, increasingly, is there a camera that will take a picture of you running a red light if you time it wrong? This moment is the zone of decision. Guess wrong, and cars crash and people get hurt or die, as thousands do every year.

"Not an exaggeration at all. You have no clue what we had to go through in our childhood. I remember the time she drove behind a bus and stopped at every bus stop along the way because she was too afraid to pass the bus into the faster traffic."

"I remember that, I remember that!" Albert struggled to spit the words out in between laughing fits.

My mother looked straight into my eyes and said: "At least, my dear, I have a driving licence." All the laughter died in the room. I said in my head: "I don't have a driving licence, but I do know how to drive." But that would be running the yellow light and crashing into a truck. That is the problem with mothers. They know you too well. They have witnessed your formative years. They have seen you on the assembly line. They have touched the naked chassis, before a protective shell had been placed on top. They know exactly where to strike in order to injure. Your only saving grace is that they love you and therefore they don't go for the kill—usually.

Airbag

THIS MORNING ON the bus I saw a woman deal admirably with an unwanted touch. She held the man's hand up in the air and broadcast her voice across the moving vehicle: "Does anyone own this hand? Does anyone own this hand?" And when she felt comfortable that she had everybody's attention she announced: "Only I found it on my bum!" The man's face turned cherry bomb red and he got off the bus at the next stop. The whole bus erupted in laughter the second he stepped out. Everybody cheered and clapped their hands. The young woman at the center of this attention took a bow to acknowledge the applause. Which only got the crowd more revved up. I joined in the festivities. It was a rare moment of temporary community togetherness. For a few minutes we stopped being individuals tolerating each other on our way

towards a destination, we became a group that is part of something bigger that was uniting us all. It felt good. I was elated when I got off the bus. It's moments like these that I will miss when I am no longer riding the bus daily to work. Hopefully! Soon. My driving test is next Tuesday. Wish me luck.

On our third wedding anniversary, I suggested to Ismail that we should take a holiday to Mexico. It would be in lieu of our honeymoon. I always felt a bit deprived because we didn't have a honeymoon. Ismail said that he didn't like being a tourist. But, I made a super cute face at him and begged him: "Please, please pleeeeeeeeeeease." Then I reminded him that this would mean avoiding Christmas in English speaking North America. We would get away from the annoying carols at the mall, the obnoxious decoration and all that forced fake good cheer that Ismail loathed. Plus no Christmas dinner with my family. I arranged the whole thing. Found an all-inclusive resort that fitted our budget and booked the flights. The heat in Puerta Vallarta is enough to delight every joint in your body. The all-encompassing heat. It was snowing back home. We boarded the airplane wearing winter jackets. We exited the airport in Mexico with the sun scolding us like a long-spurned lover itching for revenge.

I just loved playing tourist in Mexico. The beach, the swimming pool and the drinks with little umbrellas in them. Every muscle in my body was swerving with delight. Ismail, on the other hand, was miserable. One morning I joined him for breakfast to find him visibly shaken. "What happened?" I asked as I sat beside him. "I was sitting here all by myself," he said after a long pause. "I was watching all the waiters interacting with each other. The way they are warm with each other. There is a sense of community. The way they all hug when greeting each other. The way they joke around with each other. I suddenly feel intensely homesick."

"We're going home in ten days," I said.

"No not that home," he said. "I miss Morocco. I miss my family. I miss being in a place where people treat each other with humanity. In the west, everybody is focused on his little world. His job. His girlfriend. Buying some new appliance. In Morocco there is a warm social life. People are happy to see each other. You don't understand. I have lived abroad for so long, I sometimes forget how warm life can be. I am not talking about weather. I am talking about human warmth that comes from feeling connected to others."

I didn't have anything to say to him. I wanted to say: "Just relax and enjoy yourself. You are being too serious." I realize now that he needed comforting. At that moment I felt irritated with him for ruining the happy buzz I felt. It didn't help that several people at the resort assumed that he was Mexican. The staff would start speaking to him in Spanish. Ismail would explain that he didn't speak the language. The conversation would switch to English after an apology. Several guests at the resort assumed that Ismail was a

waiter. They would ask him to bring them a drink or pick up their dirty dishes.

I don't want you to think that Ismail is all doom and gloom all the time. He does have a light-hearted side. He does this thing. A goofy thing. He loves chewing gum. He has the ability to spit the gum while walking and then kick it like a football. Each time he did that he would look at me to see if I was impressed with his mouth to foot coordination. Like a twelve year old boy impressing his buddies. I miss his goofy grin.

At work today, right before lunch, Chris stood in the hallway adjacent to my cubicle screaming at nobody in particular: "I can't work with Car anymore. I can't work with Car." Then he left and didn't come back. It was the talk of the whole office. The big question lingered in the air: will he come back? Is this the end of Chris?

Sam gave me a hug and said: "I hope this means that it's over."

Cheryl said: "What a primadonna!"

Stephanie said: "Don't worry, nobody blames you." In my experience you know you are in trouble when you hear that.

Bianca said: "Good riddance."

Judy said: "Let's go out for a drink to celebrate."

My mom, ever the practical one, asked: "What if he shows up at the office with a shotgun? How much security is there at the office building?"

In truth I felt a mixture of emotions. I felt sad that Chris left a job he clearly loved. I was relieved I wouldn't have to put up with his screaming anymore. I also felt guilty for feeling relieved. It seems wrong to be happy at the misfortune of other people. I am not a member of the Secret Society of Weirdos after all.

Road Rash

I GOT DOWN ON MY knees and prayed. Yes you heard that right. I got down on my knees and prayed to God that I pass my driving test. I was in my bedroom, nobody could see me. I haven't prayed in years. Not since attending the Opera Carmen. It was a test. "Let's see if God is real," type exercise.

David showed up smiling. He opened the door for me and bowed down in an exaggerated gesture of chivalry as I got behind the steering wheel and then closed the door for me. As soon as he sat next to me I could tell there was something wrong. His left leg was shaking up and down. In all my previous 16 driving tests, David had been supportive. He would shower me with reassuring statements such as: "You got this!" or "You are a good driver, just believe in yourself." This time he sat next to me fidgeting and said

nothing. I was a ball of nerves as I drove to the DMV office. My palms were sweaty. My stomach was grumbling. I couldn't help notice David's unusual behavior. "Are you ok?" I asked him. "I am fine, just pay attention to driving," he said.

I was sitting in my car waiting for the examiner. An older man showed up with the usual clipboard. He looked like a younger version of Sylvester. "This is a good omen," I thought. My whole body was shaking from the nervous energy that was radiating up and down my spine. I was trying to focus on breathing to calm myself down but it wasn't working. The examiner sat in the passenger seat next to me, fastened his seat belt and said: "Start the engine and turn left on the main road up ahead." I took a deep breath and did as instructed. My hands were visibly shaking while holding the steering wheel. I drove straight ahead for several minutes, waiting for further instructions. The examiner said nothing, so I just kept driving forwards. I passed a supermarket, a commercial center, a bunch of buildings. I stopped at a stop sign while a mother pushing a baby carriage in front of her crossed the street. The silence in the car was eerie. I took a glance at the examiner only to realize that he was sleeping. Hence the quiet and lack of instructions. "Perfect! I will let him sleep. Drive around a bit. By the time we return to the DMV he will feel too embarrassed for snoozing on the job, he will be forced to pass me." A massive wave of calm descended on me. My hands were as steady as steel. I drove around the neighbourhood enjoying myself. The realization dawned on me that I had conquered my fright of driving tests. "I am a fantastic driver!" The thought plopped into my mind. "It's not driving that I am afraid of, it's being

judged that sends my nerves into the shredder. I don't need to learn how to drive, I need to learn how to not care what others think of me." This insight is worth gold. I felt happy to be in command of the metaphorical steering wheel of my life. "Yes! Yes! I finally get what is ailing me. I am buying the beautiful pistachio green Nissan Juke tomorrow." I drove back to the DMV, parked the car and said a polite "ehm!" to wake up the examiner. He didn't budge. I coughed. Nothing. No reaction. Then hacked like an old smoker. Still nothing happened. I finally poked his forearm with my finger. His hand fell lifelessly to the side.

I gasped.

I ran into the office shrieking: "Help! Help! Something happened to the examiner."

People ran out, and soon an ambulance arrived. My examiner was declared dead on the spot by the paramedics.

"Don't you think I should be getting a pass?" I asked David on our way home. He was driving.

"The man died and all you care about is your stupid driving license?" asked David, angrily.

"What is wrong with you today! It's not like I killed him." I snapped back.

"The man died and you continued to take the test. You could've saved his life by checking on him earlier." David parked in front of my apartment building.

"I thought he was sleeping," I said. I had both the palms of my hand on my face. A double face palm.

David started crying. His whole body shook with the heaving.

"You have ruined my life. I had a perfect driving instructor record until I met you. I used to tell people that 100% of my students received their driving license. I can't say that anymore."

His whining reminded me of C-3PO from Star Wars.

"But David! Today I had a realization. A big Aha moment. I know why I failed all the other tests. I finally know how to pass it. That is a happy thing, no?" I was certain this would cheer him up, but I was wrong.

"I don't care. My ex is not allowing me a visit with my son. All you women are the same. Just get out of my car. I don't ever want to see you again," David said in between sobs.

I got out of his car to watch him drive off. That was it, I never heard or saw David again.

I seem to have this effect on men. They want to be around me for a while and then they can't stand being around me all of a sudden. I am a man repellent.

I didn't hear or see Chris either for the next two months after his dramatic exit from the office. My work progressed well and things seemed to be going peachy with the documentation. After two months of blissful, shout-free work days, Chris walked into the office and headed straight to the meeting room. My boss's boss, the R&D director of the company, looked like he was expecting the

unexpected visitor and got up from his desk and walked into the meeting room as well, closing the door behind him. "Oh no! Chris will ask for his job back!" a sense of dread filled me. I could feel my heart beats speeding inside my chest. "O! breathe Car, breathe!" I told myself. "I can deal with this, I have dealt with it before, breathe in, breathe out, stay calm ... don't panic." I closed my eyes and tried to imagine a beautiful lush garden with water fountains and roaming peacocks. That didn't work. So imagined comical looking cars with horns sticking out the roofs. After about 45 minutes, my boss's boss walked out of the meeting room with Chris following him.

"Hey Car, come over here, Chris has something to tell you." I got up from my seat and faced Chris who proceeded to say: "I am deeply sorry for my past behavior. I now realize that I was rude and offensive. I don't deserve your forgiveness but please forgive me." I was taken by surprise, I had never expected Chris to apologize. "Oh Chris, this is great! I accept your apology," I said, nearly jumping up and down. "Let us put the past behind us, water under the bridge, and forge ahead with new camaraderie." Chris looked happy with my response and traces of a smile showed on his face. I felt encouraged some more and I said "To seal this new friendship, hey how about we go for lunch together?"

Chris said "that's great, when?"

"Next Wednesday!" I said. "I am so happy that we sorted this out, to make it official, lets shake hands on it. "I extended my hand towards Chris. Chris grabbed my hand, but instead of shaking it, he raised my hand towards his face and placed a gentle kiss on the back of it. Then his eyes teared up, and he looked all emotional.

Suddenly, he let go of my hand and stormed out of the office without saying a word. I felt touched: "Oooo, he was sincere in his apology," I thought to myself. "He wasn't just saying it to get his job back. He really meant it."

That is when my boss's boss started to laugh. He was laughing so hard that he was holding his stomach and bending over like somebody who is afraid he might bust a hernia. "Now I know what was going on," he repeated a few times.

"It is obvious what was going on," I said defiantly. "His ego was bruised because he was losing control over the project that was his baby, he projected all that anxiety onto a lowly technical writer."

"That is what I used to think was going on, but now I realize that something else was going on," my boss's boss said while still laughing hysterically.

"Ok, genius!" I said. "Why don't you explain it me then."

"Car," my boss's boss said in a soft voice, looking intently into my eyes. "Chris is in love with you, he was in there asking me for advice on how to ask you out on a date." My eyes widened with shock. Turns out Chris was not asking for his job back and I just suggested having lunch with him. "Oh no! Oh no!" I shook my head with denial. "But that is not what I meant!" I exclaimed. "I know what you meant" said my boss. "But I am just letting you know that there is something else going on, so I leave it up to you to decide how to proceed." Needless to say, I cancelled my lunch appointment with Chris via email.

After that I received flowers and gifts from him at the office, which always triggered a hysterical laugh from Stephanie and a

concerned look from me. Cheryl and Sam seemed amused by the whole thing. I liked Chris so much better when he hated my guts and told me that I was the most stupid person on earth. I knew how to react to that, but I wasn't sure how to handle this new incarnation. In hind sight, I suppose the little red x marks on the map were meant as a romantic gesture, which I had foolishly interpreted as an insult.

If I was a car, I would be the type of car that has no wheels, no doors, no transmission, no engine, no seats and no body. I would be a carless car. More like a car concept before the internal combustion engine was invented. I am like an idea in the mind of a German peasant who is riding a horse driven cart and dreaming about a flying carpet while thinking about how nice it would be if his cart would magically move itself without the darn four legged creature he must feed. I am nothing. Oh yes, I know that I have two legs that move me around. A body that hosts my being and a mind which directs my actions. But lately as I walk around the clean streets of this beautiful city with hands in my pockets, I can't shake the feeling that I hardly exist at all. As if a tiny percentage of myself was in the here and now and the rest of me is scattered in the hidden recesses of the universe where the astronauts dream that one day their grandchildren will reach. My subtracted state is fooling everybody.

Even my own mother whose vagina had expelled me into this world doesn't notice that most of my substance has drained into a lifeless gutter. I suppose I shouldn't feel so bad. After all nothing holds the potential for everything. A carless car is better that a car accident. A concept is pregnant with potential that no reality can possibly fulfil. Empty of myself I go through my daily routine holding a memory of the things that the full Car used to do. The full Car got up at 7, reached the office at 8:13 and sat quietly at her desk to check her email at precisely 8:16 am. And so the empty car remembers and imitates. "If it was the right thing to do back then, then it must be the right thing to do now." I must go on going on. What choice do I have? .... stop? crash? self-destruct? blow-up? ..... or set myself on fire?

I wasn't always so nothing. Just last year the trunk of my life was full to the brim with people and interactions. No sooner was our wedding over, than Ismail had turned our apartment into what I affectionately called free bed and breakfast. Marriage to Ismail meant marrying a revolving door of rag tag strangers that were invited to stay with us. The near homeless, recent immigrants with nowhere to stay and battered wives were but a sample of people staying in our free bed and breakfast. My apartment now stays empty. If anybody was in need, Ismail would invite them to stay in the second

bedroom with us. Together we would feed and nurse our guest or guests, counsel them, drive them around and generally help them get up on their feet again. Ismail works as a journeyman in a lumber mill. But this merely is his means of earning a living to pay the rent. His true vocation, which he performs for free and has no official training for, is social worker. Ismail has this magical ability to insert himself into the life of the most random of random strangers. Tweak around, say the right words, make a few arrangements and Kaboom! That person's life is transformed. From ash-covered Cinderella to the belle of the ball. People entered our apartment downtrodden, barely able to speak for themselves and walked out our door, a few months later, singing: *I Will Survive* by Gloria Gaynow. He is the grown up male version of Pippi Longstocking, minus the red hair braids. I had one rule, which Ismail accepted: no junkies. Otherwise I threw myself heart and soul into Ismail's quest to right all social wrongs he encountered.

Soukaina came to live with us with a new born baby girl and a two year old Mohammed. First there were furtive phone calls in the middle of the night with Soukaina whispering and crying on the other end. On those nights, Ismail was calm and reassuring, speaking to her over the phone in a comforting tone. Then one day after such a phone call, I could hear Ismail saying: "Just wait for me downstairs, I am coming right now." It was 2 a.m. I was annoyed that my sleep was interrupted yet again. Ismail jumped out of bed. He grabbed his car keys and went out the door. Thirty minutes later he walked back in with Soukaina and her children with nothing but the clothes on their back and a large bag of diapers. Without any

introductions or formality Ismail directed them to the spare
bedroom. He asked me to set up the extra mattresses we had on the
floor for the children. Once I was done with that, he instructed me
to go to bed to let our guests rest. Once Ismail joined me I finally
got to find out what was going on. He sighed deeply and told me
how Hamza (Soukaina's husband) had been violent with her recently
and she had nowhere else to go. The next day I found Soukaina in
my kitchen, having prepared breakfast for everybody. Coffee, toast
and boiled eggs. I also couldn't help notice that she washed the dirty
dishes piled up in the sink and wiped down the counters. For a
battered wife she sure had lots of extra energy. Ismail looked deeply
touched by the gesture. "You are our guest, we should make
breakfast for you," he said with his hand over his chest. Soukaina
smiled shyly while tucking away a stray strand of hair into her head
covering. Her limited English and my poor ass Arabic made
communicating with her a bumpy ride. Ismail frequently acted like a
translator. When I came home from work that night I discovered
that she had vacuumed the carpets, did the laundry, and cooked
lamb tagine from whatever she found in my fridge. I thanked
Soukaina for her effort and told her that it wasn't necessary. She
smiled back sweetly saying: "Apartment very dirty, must clean." I
smiled back, disguising my irritation. This woman proceeded to take
over my humble apartment. She cleaned, cooked and did my
laundry, yes even my dirty underwear. She was the most annoying
person to ever stay with us. She made me feel like a total failure as a
wife and a woman. I wanted to scream at her: "Stop cleaning, stop
cooking, this is my apartment!" Ismail, on the other hand, was

delighted with her cooking and he was clearly delighted with having Mohammed and the baby girl around. He came home with little toys for Mohammed showering him with hugs and fatherly affection. Had you walked into our home during Soukaina's reign you would have assumed that I was the guest intruding on the residing family. Ismail was all chatter and laughter around the dinner table. Soukaina was serving the food. Mohammed was jumping around. Baby girl was sucking her thumb. One big happy Moroccan family. I didn't belong in the picture. Soukaina didn't have anything and yet I felt jealous of her. After two weeks, we discovered that she was afraid of leaving the apartment on her own. Hamza had convinced her that it was dangerous. So we encouraged her to go for walks with the kids. We went to the bank with her to open a bank account in her name. Then Ismail arranged for her to get social assistance. One night we were sitting after dinner, and Soukaina said that baby girl had slept through the night. Ismail said: "good girl!" And then he suggested to Soukaina that she should choose a name for her baby. Soukaina teared up: "What if I choose a name that Hamza disapproves of?" Ismail looked moved by her tears. I sat next to her and gave her a hug. Ismail said: "Hamza isn't here, I think you should choose a name." Mohammed jumped up and down saying: "We should name her after Auntie Car." Soukaina smiled at her son and said: "I always wanted to have a daughter that I called Iman." Ismail clapped his hands in approval. "Iman it is!" I cooed at the baby in Soukaina's hands.

Once the welfare checks began to arrive, we busied ourselves searching for an apartment for Soukaina. Finally I had the idea to

ask Soukaina what she would like to do professionally. Soukaina's eyes widened and she inhaled deeply: "Nobody ever asked me that."

"I am asking now," I said.

"I always wanted to be a hairdresser," she whispered. I researched a nearby college that offered an eight month certificate in hairdressing. Classes run three days a week. Soukaina pointed at Mohammed and Iman. "What about them? Who will take care of them while I go to school?" I told her we would figure it out. I enrolled Soukaina in the classes myself. Ismail and I agreed to take care of the kids on Saturday. And we hired a next door neighbour to watch the kids the other two days. Soukaina began to flourish. She had a new air of confidence about her. Half way through her studies we managed to rent a one bedroom apartment for her. We helped her move, bought some basic furniture. Soukaina secured a job at a big hair salon in a shopping mall. I watched Soukaina transform herself from a woman who was afraid to go outside on her own into a strong independent woman that was managing her own affairs. I was relieved when they moved out and my apartment was my own again. I think Soukaina was Ismail's greatest accomplishment. The Porsche of his fleet of people he has transformed.

Looking back at it I can see how I missed all the obvious clues that Ismail desired a family. Every cell in his body was screaming: "Make me a father!" I didn't see it because I didn't want to. I am 32 years old. Shouldn't my biological clock be ticking? I can't feel a thing. Not even a twinge.

Not all of Ismail's efforts at social change were as successful as Soukaina. Brain was a homeless person we found in a park one August night. That is not a typo. He insisted that his name was Brain, like the organ inside your head. Ismail and I were holding hands while taking a leisurely walk. I was admiring the red, orange and green colors in the trees and about to tell Ismail: "Do you know who is the best artist in the world?" I was planning to pause and let him guess and then answer with: "Fall. Fall is the the greatest artist in the entire world." But before I had the chance to utter this philosophical gem, Ismail abruptly dropped my hand and went running towards a dark corner next to the concession stand. Brain had set up his sleeping bag underneath the awning to spend the night. Brain looked alarmed by our presence.

"Are you guys Christians?" He asked, stretching out the words like chewing gum.

"No we we are not Christian, we are not trying to convince you of any religion at all," replied Ismail.

"What do you want then?" Brain had a smirk on his face that bore the mark of somebody who others have attempted to save too many times.

"We would like to offer you a place to stay the night. For free. With no strings attached," Ismail said.

Ismail and I helped Brain gather up his few belongings and we walked over to our apartment. After he took a shower I invited Brain to sit down at the dinning table to have something to eat. I made him a turkey breast sandwich.

"My name is Brain because I am very smart," he said, lifting an index finger in the air in my direction to emphasize the point.

"I assumed it was Brian and you decided to switch is around a bit," I said while placing cheese and cold cuts back in the fridge.

"Is that what you did with your name? You are Carmen and decided to switch it around?"

"No!" I shouted with my head stuck in the fridge.

"See I am smart, that is why I am Brain. You can't fool me. I have read everything that Dostoyevsky has written twice." He pointed two fingers in the air to indicate the number two.

"No kidding?" I said, sitting at the dining table across from him.

"Yes, yes, yes, ask me anything. Anything at all. I bet I know the answer," he said with a mouth full of mangled sandwich.

"Ok, What is love?" I was sure to stump him with that one.

"In The Brothers Karamazov Dostoyevsky asks 'What is hell? I maintain that it is the suffering of being unable to love.' Deducing from that, I would say that love is a glimpse of heaven that you get as a result of a connection you form with another person."

I was speechless. I have to admit that this is best definition of love I ever heard. Brain and I sat silent across from each other as I watched him chomp down the sandwich. Having Brain stay with us was completely different from Soukaina. He never cleaned after

himself. The guest bedroom was so messy that it was dangerous to step into it for fear you might step on something or something might fall on your head. And he never ever cooked. Which was just fine by me. Brain was resistant to any and all suggestions that Ismail made. The list included:

"I can help you find a job."

"I can help you find your own apartment."

"I can look into applying for social assistance."

"I can help you get in touch with your family."

Brain's answer to everything was "No, thank you." He didn't explain or elaborate. He simply didn't want us to help him with anything. He didn't want improvement of his lot of any kind. In fact he looked happy. He sung in the shower. Hummed to himself in the bedroom. He never complained about the food I served him. He never complimented me on my cooking either. Never said thank you or showed gratitude. Didn't tell us anything about himself or his past. Talking about novels was his favorite topic. In the evening he sat to read one of the books from our bookshelves. I could tell that Ismail was irritated with Brain. I enjoyed watching the dynamic. Brain was my revenge for Soukaina. I delighted in Ismail's exasperation.

As December rolled around, Brain complained that there was no Christmas tree in our place. I explained to him that Ismail and I didn't celebrate Christmas. "What's the point of being a family if you don't celebrate Christmas?" he asked. To appease him I bought a mini fake Christmas tree. The kind that you can place on a table. A sort of a half measure. I called Albert to ask If I could bring Brain

to the family Christmas dinner. Albert made it clear that Christmas is for family. His exact words were: "I respect Ismail for sheltering the homeless. He is a better man than I am. However, your current charity case is not invited to the family gathering." Ismail felt insulted that we couldn't bring Brain with us. "That is typical western Christmas spirit. Generosity to everybody except the ones who actually need it." We agreed we would have a mini Christmas dinner with Brain before we left to be with extended family. I cooked salmon and pasta. We bought Brain a matching knitted green hat, green scarf and green mittens which I presented to him with a festive card. Brian opened his gift and said that he didn't like green. But he wore all three items anyway. Brain didn't seem to appreciate that I had made a special effort just for him. Which felt hurtful. We spent three nights at my brothers house and returned home.

On New Year's day, I woke up before Ismail, and went to the kitchen to make coffee. Two hands materialized out of thin air and I felt a body pressed to my behind. When I looked around it was Brain. I pushed him away and screamed: "Don't touch me!" "Hey! Shh s sh" He waved the palms of his hands in my face but spoke in a whisper: "Don't wake up your husband."

"What were you doing?" I mouthed the words.

"I need sex," He whispered back, pointing at his crotch. "I have human needs like every man. Food and shelter is not enough. I also need sex." His eyes widened.

"That's not my problem." My hands where in front of me to shield me from any further advances.

"You made me your problem when you invited me to live with you," he said. "We can do it on the sly. Your man never has to find out." Brain smiled leerily.

I didn't know what to say. I simply walked out of the kitchen and back to my bedroom. When I told Ismail what happened, he was seething with anger. He stayed in the bedroom until he calmed himself down. Then he went to Brain's bedroom and told him:

"You need to collect your things and move out today."

"You need to learn to share," Brain said, staring at the finger Ismail was pointing at him. It made him go cross eyed.

"I shared with you my home, my food." The index finger turned into a fist.

"Why can't you share your wife? You think you are generous, but you are begrudging me that."

Ismail didn't argue with him. He repeated: "You need to move out today."

And that was the end of our story with Brain.

Yesterday Hakeem invited me over for dinner at his place to introduce me properly to his new wife, Farida. I arrived holding hot cross buns. Farida smiled revealing beautiful white teeth as she took them off my hands. Over chicken tagine and couscous, I asked Farida how she liked her life in our beautiful city. Farida smiled at Hakeem and he smiled back. You could feel the electric energy between them. Perhaps arranged marriage isn't so bad. Hakeem patiently translated all my questions and then her answers. When we finished eating I complimented Farida on her cooking: "This was so good!" Farida said: "Hakeem says that you are a good cook."

I gave Hakeem a surprised look. "He has perjured himself most profoundly."

Hakeem smiled: "Ok, maybe you are not a good cook. But I do miss the good old days when your house was the gathering spot for any Moroccan who had nowhere to go. Your generosity was most astounding."

"It wasn't me, it was Ismail's doing," I said, sighing. "Surely all who are in need are pounding on his new door." I said.

"Oh no! Fatin has put her foot down and forbidden Ismail from bringing any strangers to her home. The Moroccan community needs a new mayor." Haleem waved his hand.

Hakeem's words bore through my heart like a tank. I always assumed that helping Ismail with his social work was a non-negotiable part of his identity. It was the definition of who he was. It never occurred me that saying no was even an option. I totally feel like a member of The Secret Society of Wierdos from Da Falihi Can story now.

Sunroof

SOME LIFT THEIR eyesight up to the sky for inspiration. Stargazing at night fills them with awe at God's creation. I find no such solace. Instead I enjoy looking down. From the sky down to earth. In my dreams I imagine I am watching cities from an airplane window. Some cities are quietly competent, like Berlin or Detroit. Others beam up a boiling energy that reverberates in my body, like New York or Hong Kong. And then I imagine Paris or Istanbul, they move the heart with mega-watt charisma. I love looking out the window from a tall building. Watching people and vehicles intermingle is like seeing musical patterns. This must be what God sees when he looks down at us.

Cities are living beings. One day when I have the money to travel I shall go to all these cities and experience it for myself. After

I encounter them from far above, once I land, I would like to find those main streets and highways that structure their space. Especially at night, commuters make these arteries look mystically red and golden. The city's vascular system performing its vital function right before my eyes. Each city has hidden corners that you can discover by chance. Beautiful parts. Touristy parts. And then ugly parts. The underbelly that is hidden away. It can take a life time to familiarize yourself with the pulse of a city. But I am a fast learner. It takes me one year to truly understand a city. My secret is simple: walking. I point at a random location on a map, go there and then wander off. Walk wherever my feet will take me. I notice the concrete beneath my feet. Scraps of disjointed conversations overheard as I pass by people talking to each other. I register the speed of the cars driving by. The subtle mannerisms of traffic maneuvering. The way people honk at each other or flicker their headlights at each other to demand attention. I allow all these impressions to seep in and over time a collage of sights, sounds, smells and random words provides me with a map to this giant beast whose bowels I am living in. I used to feel proud of my ability to get under the skin of any city I moved to. My ability to transform myself from visitor to a native seemed exceptional. But now I doubt my abilities. I thought that I knew the inner map of Ismail. I walked along those cobblestone roads leading directly to his heart. Studied the urban planning of his imagination and familiarized myself with every obscure corner of his psyche. Clearly I was wrong. The illusion of my intimacy with him came to a violent crashing halt the day the divorce papers arrived by courier at my door.

Today, I didn't want to gaze at my city. There was a sports match, and the local team had lost. This led to riots and looting in the downtown area. The scenery from the bus stop to the office resembled a war zone. Vehicles on fire, smashed glass and garbage everywhere. In the midst of all this carnage there was a middle-aged woman dressed as a Brazilian samba dancer calmly stepping over the debris in her bejeweled shiny shoes, pink feathers sticking out of her behind and a headpiece that seemed to be inspired by some ancient culture. She looked as if a hurricane had just scooped her up from the Rio De Janeiro Carnival and placed her inside this setting as a joke. A shiver buzzed through my spine as I rushed towards the safety of the office. I had lived in this city my whole life. I thought I knew it. Understood it. I am an alien in my own birth place! Hiding from the outside world, I stepped into cubicle land hoping to capture a sense of bland normalcy. I thought I was the first one in. The lights weren't on. I kept them off. I left my handbag at my desk and headed towards the kitchen to grab a cup of coffee. In the semi-dark I saw Cheryl kneeling beside the opened fridge. Her face was illuminated by the appliance's light. She was placing all the cartons of milk into a large canvas bag. I couldn't believe it. Cheryl is the office milk thief! I would have never guessed. This day is full of bad omens.

Then around 10:00, I was summoned to Stephanie's office and informed that I was being laid off. Stephanie got the orders of the big shot CTO who had visited us three months earlier. He instructed every department head to reduce staff by 20% three days after RemoteSenseTX was complete. "But why me?" I asked her. "You could have chosen Sam or Cheryl!"

Stephanie didn't give me an answer. She was all vague, saying things like: "It was a difficult choice. I had no say in the matter." I felt tempted to tell her that Cheryl was the milk thief. But then I decided that she wouldn't believe me. I was escorted to my desk by a security guard, instructed to gather my things and then led outside while bewildered Cheryl and Sam looked on. Others from each department were on the street carrying boxes as well. We avoided looking at each other. The city was beginning to recover. The burning vehicle was now smoldering. Smashed windows were already replaced and businesses were open for business. There was still debris along the sidewalk. I headed home, dropped my box next to Ismail's boxes filled with books in my closet and went out to see a mid-day matinee at a nearby theater. *Beauty And The Beast* was playing. Not the animated one, the live action one starring Emma Watson. I thought it would cheer me up. One block away from the movie theater, I saw Joshua walking out of a coffee shop talking on the phone. Right behind him walked a second Joshua, only this one looked like the Joshua I had met on the first date. Long haired, with an earring dangling from one earlobe. I had to pause for a few seconds to register what I was seeing. They are twins. They have been playing a sick prank on me all along. The clean shaven Joshua

jumped back when he saw me. But I just walked right past him and into the theater without a word. I didn't care what he had to say. Luckily the cinema was dark and empty. I could cry to my heart's content without obstruction. Let the history books record, this wasn't the shittiest day in my life. I can remember a worse one.

For three months I was convinced that Ismail was either kidnapped or detained against his will. Yes, the note he left on the dinning table was in his handwriting, but surely he wrote it under duress. I imagined he wrote it to protect me from harm. I made up a story in my mind that a violent group of criminals had kidnapped him to force him into collaborating with the robbery. They threatened to kill me if he didn't go along with their plan. And so poor Ismail wrote that note to protect me from harm while he was on a *Mission Impossible* type adventure. I imagined a mafioso type called Gragis who was bold, wore expensive suits and spoke in a soft hissy voice. Gragis would be an international bank robber who has evaded capture for 15 years. He would be famous for his meticulous planning ahead of each job and for carefully picking a team hand crafted to suit each mission. Gragis had set his sight on an eccentric Belgian billionaire who kept a treasure trove of diamonds in a vault installed in a cave high up on the Jungfrau mountain. The cave is protected by hungry roaming grizzly bears that make accessing it

nearly impossible. Gragis had hired an expert bear hunter from South Africa. A highly trained helicopter pilot from the Philippines. Three expert rock climbers from Azerbaijan. And then he needed to recruit a vault breaker. An old contact gave him the name of Ismail Harrak. Little did Gragis know that there are probably 20,000 Moroccans called Ismail Harrak in the world. And that the vault breaker Ismail Harrak wasn't my Ismail Harrak. Now my poor Honey Hubcap was being held hostage and has to figure out how to break into a one of a kind safe after a hazardous climb up the mountain where he could be mauled by a grizzly bear.

I went to the police with my theory. I didn't tell them about Gragis and the mountain vault. Just that I was concerned with my husband's well being. The lovely police officer listened to me patiently. His eyes where blue and sympathetic. He explained to me that husbands leave their wives all the time. Although walking away with only a note is cowardly, it's not illegal. "The police can't get involved in personal strife," he said.

When talking to the police failed, I went to our friends. Well! What used to be our friends. But now I realize they were Ismail's friends who tolerated me on his account. I met with Hisham and his wife Abeer. Both kept looking at each other as I told them about Ismail's disappearance. I tried to convince them that they needed to help me rescue him since, the police were refusing to do their job. Hisham inhaled loudly and then said nothing. Abeer made strange gestures with her head which I couldn't decipher. Next I went to visit Tarik and Amira.

I had spent five nights staring at the ceiling when the thought occurred to me that I should go visit Hakeem. I had always liked him. I called him to let him know that I needed to see him right away. I called a taxi. In my rush to get to my destination, I made the mistake of sitting in the passenger seat next to the driver. The traffic was unusually busy for 7pm.

"Why is it so busy?" I asked. I wasn't myself which explains why I started the conversation.

"The game, it's tonight, everybody is expecting to celebrate afterwards," said the taxi driver.

"I guess you don't care about sports," he said when I didn't respond. "But surely your husband does."

"My husband doesn't." I shook my head.

"Strange. Where is he from?" He threw me a glance sideways. I looked out the window to avoid meeting his eyes.

"Morocco," I said. In a car to my right a couple was fighting. The woman was yelling and gesturing with her hands. The man behind the steering wheel was rolling his eyes. Their car sped past us leaving behind streaks of discontent.

"I see!" Said the driver, smiling.

"What do you mean?" I held the roof handle bar with my right hand.

"Nothing. It just explains something I was wondering about." He continued to smile.

"So tell me," I said, sitting back in my seat.

"Are you sure you want to know?" He clicked his tongue after.

"Spit it out already." I rolled my eyes.

"I was surprised to see a wedding ring on your finger, because you don't look like the type." He laughed the way a villain in a super hero movie might laugh, making an ar ar ar sound. It sounded fake.

"The type?" I repeated.

"The type that settles for one man. But we all know that North African men are good in bed. So that explains why you are married." More ar ar ar laughing.

"What a load of crap!" I looked through the sun roof to catch a glimpse of the sky. Why must I always get the lunatics?

"See! I knew you would deny it." He shrugged his shoulders.

"There is nothing to deny. Marriage is not about sex." I sighed.

"Tell that to somebody else. Your husband is good in bed. Am I right or wrong?" He cackled as if about to destroy the world with a nuclear bomb.

"That is none of your business."

"There is nothing wrong with it. You white chicks love the sex. Hurray! Women's liberation." His eye brows moved up and down. Bushy eye brows too.

"I can't believe what I am hearing. Must you manifest every immigrant cliché during this ride?"

"You look sexually satisfied. I am happy for you. All women deserve that." His eye brows were having a conversation with each other. The left brow and right brow were moving up, down, right and left in a dance configuration.

We were stuck in traffic. And this wacko taxi driver was going on about my supposed sex life. As much as I love traffic gazing, moments like these can make life tilt into hellish hues. Nothing can make this better. Not public radio. Not mindful meditation. All the deep breaths in the world. Being stuck in traffic with a boorish asshole is the worst punishment in the world.

From there I went to see Hakeem, who was still single at the time. Hakeem looked compassionately into my eyes and advised me to go home and get some rest. He got up, picked up a book from his book shelf and handed it to me, saying: "I read this when I was having a hard time and it helped me." It was *Eat. Pray. Love* by Elizabeth Gilbert.

The idea came to me as I was lying in bed staring at the ceiling wondering what I could do to rescue my husband. I needed to call Ismail's boss at work. Perhaps his employer would be willing to take responsibly for his employee. I spoke to Tom first thing the next morning.

"What?" Shouted Tom over a mechanical buzz in the background.

"Good morning." I said after clearing my throat.

"What can I do for you?" The background noise went down.

"My name is Car. I am Ismail's wife," I said. My hands were shaking as I spoke. My voice wavering.

"Ismail has started his shift, he can't come to the phone," Tom said, still shouting even though I could hear him fine. I moved the phone an inch away from my ear.

"He can't be at work, he has been kidnapped!" I said.

"Fuck you! I don't have time for your shit-face pranks,"

He slammed down the phone. My indignation at the insult gave way to the realization that Ismail was at work. And if Ismail was at work, that means he hadn't been kidnapped. He was missing from my life by his own choice. I would say that was the worst day in my life. The most horrid moment in my armored car of memories. It taught me that I can't trust my mind. If I can't trust my mind and I can't trust my heart, then what can I trust?

Empty Tank

ONE WEEK AGO I received a memorial service announcement in my mailbox. I was sad to discover that my bus buddy Sylvester had died. On the day of the funeral, I wore a black skirt, gray blouse and a gray jacket. The bus that got me there was relatively empty. There were maybe two other passengers on board. Life in the unemployed lane was looking good. I leaned my forehead against the window and resolved to stare at everything. Right as we were on the bridge, a motorcycle passed us. A large young woman was holding the waist of the motorcycle driver. Both of them were wearing helmets so I couldn't see their faces. Half her ass was hanging out of her pants, plumber style. A butt crack and two half bulging cheeks for all the world to see. I guess she desperately needed to adjust her clothing to cover up but too afraid to let go to do it. How I wished I could've

laughed. Why does this hilarious thing happen on a day when I am feeling blue? Even better would've been to share it with passengers around me. "Hey look at that!" I would point out to a stranger next to me and we would laugh together. A moment of connection. I arrived at the synagogue precisely on time. A rather impressive accomplishment given the fact that I took the bus. At the doorway stood Ariel, Sylvester's son and the one who sent me the memorial service notice. Ariel is a middle-aged man with greying hair sprouting around his temple. He looked dignified and somber. I shook his hand and introduced myself, then I offered my condolences. I stepped inside and sat in the third row. I was surprised by how modern the main sanctuary looked. The stained glass windows looked like they were inspired by Miro. The main hall was round giving it a warm, cozy feeling. Within twenty minutes the front row seats had filled up. The rabbi started the service with a solemn sermon on death. That was followed by speeches from Sylvester's friends and co-workers. People talked about his work as a traffic engineer but also a whole slew of things that surprised me because I didn't know about them. One friend talked about how Sly (that seemed to be his nick name among his friends who were his own age) was a pilot and owned his own Cessna. A woman co-worker seemed to imply that Sly was into cocaine. She referred to it as white powder. Everybody in the audience laughed when she mentioned Sly's fondness for a certain white powder, except the rabbi. He knotted his eye brows and his lips scrunched up to one side. I guess this isn't the usual service held in this temple. Finally, Sly's son Ariel went up to the microphone. He thanked everybody

who had come. He hesitated a beat, and then said: "We talked about different aspects of my father's life. But there is one thing nobody mentioned. As most of you already know, my father was gay." Some people in the audience started clapping. Others remained silent. The rabbi covered his mouth as if he was stopping himself from screaming. The room started to swivel around as if it was an attraction ride. I became afraid that I would fall off my chair and onto the floor, disrupting this solemn ceremony. Ariel continued with his speech, but I couldn't hear anything that he said. I leaned over forwards, placing the palms of my hand on the edge of the seat to prevent myself from falling and focused on breathing. Closing my eyes helped the dizziness stop as well. As soon as the service was finished, I ran outside to catch the first bus, no matter its destination.

At home, I felt so agitated I picked up the phone to call my mother. She laughed when I told her the story. "But Mom! I am devastated," I said.

"Don't worry darling, there will be no revelations at my funeral that I am gay," she said. Talking with my mom didn't help, so I called Bianca and Judy. Both came over bearing wine, cheese and crackers.

"This is the last straw, I can't take any more devastation." I wiped away tears as Bianca and Judy placed the food and drink on the coffee table.

"Why is this bothering you so much?" Asked Judy. "So he was gay, so what?"

"It's not the fact the he was gay that bothers me," I said, reaching for my wine glass.

"I get it. You were friends and he didn't trust you with this information," said Bianca right before taking a sip from her glass.

"No! that's not it either. What bothers me is the fact that he told me all those stories about how much he loved his late wife. I was deeply touched by it. Why did he lie to me? He could have not talked about her at all. I would have been ok with it. Just because we were friends doesn't mean he had to disclose to me every aspect of his life. But why did he lie? I feel that everything in life is a falsehood." I took a large swig from my glass.

"Maybe you should go see somebody, seek help," said Judy.

I hate and loathe self-help books. I am embarrassed to confess that I read *The Secret* because Bianca told me it was the best thing she ever read and Judy insisted that I read it. I found it to be a bunch of gobbledygook. The summary of its essence is that I should spend my time fantasizing about expensive luxuries that I can't afford and when unfortunate events happen in my life they are all my fault because I wasn't positive enough in my thinking. Other self-help authors seem to communicate "My life is great, don't you wish you could be like me?" Apologies Mr. Self Help, I am glad that you managed to get everything sorted out in your life, but we can't

all make money selling the "I am fantastic, what is wrong with you?" message.

Therapy is not for me either. The thought of paying somebody to care about me and my problems seems fundamentally wrong. The same way paying for sex seems fundamentally wrong. Certain things in life should come for free or not come at all. If you are paying per hour for love, care and understanding, is it really love care and understanding or some perverted version that looks the same with a far more sinister undertone?

Then there is yoga. I had heard many raves about the magical, life altering powers of the downward dog and sunshine salutation. I wanted to march with the army of the faithful and join the chorus of those that sing the praises of ancient wisdom. I tried one yoga studio in my neighborhood and went faithfully twice a week. When that failed to yield any benefits, I decided to try another and another place. Fish pose, butterfly, tree pose, warrior pose, camel, lotus pose, frog, cobra, eagle, pigeon—all were attempted with dutiful effort. The only part of yoga that seemed natural was sitting cross legged on the floor, having spent time in Morocco, that part was the only one that gave me no challenge. The enchanted qualities of yoga eluded me from one studio to the next, until I had to declare defeat. Perhaps yoga does yield benefits to other people, but Car is not made for posing nor for animal impersonations. Whatever nuggets of wisdom there are to be reaped from ancient culture of India, I am yet to grasp a single gem of it.

Then there is meditation. I am not sure I know what it is, therefore I can't tell you what I think of it. I went to a group

meditation session and when I asked the instructor: "What is meditation?" everybody in the group started laughing, but no explanation was provided. I am glad I gave that group some laughter because most of the time they seemed way too serious and boring. My mind is too restless to be empty of thoughts. Furthermore, I realized that it is not in my nature to be peaceful, I am too passionate, too engaged, too curious to be a peaceful person. So whatever meditation is, I eventually gave up on it as well.

What is a woman in crisis to do when all the wisdom of the east and all the commercial vices of the west fail to provide a suitable answer? Unfortunately, yet again, I have to find my own way.

I need to get away. Given how happy I was during my trip to San Francisco, the only way for me to fix this broken heart is to travel somewhere far away. The further the better. Away from all the memories. A place where I can renew myself. I remembered the words of Sylvester on one of our bus meetings: "Lausanne, Switzerland is the smallest city in the world with a rapid transit system. It's the most efficient place on earth with regards to traffic." I hope he didn't lie about that. Sounds like exactly my place. I always have my best insights on the bus. I will travel to Lausanne, spend most of the day on the public transit. I will be swimming in insights. My version of *Eat. Pray. Love.* will be—*Ride the bus. Ride the train. Ride the subway.* I will ride all the public transit the beautiful city of Lausanne has to offer until my broken heart is healed.

Windshield

SPLAT! One mosquito down, 38 more to go. My copy of *Eat. Pray. Love* by Elizabeth Gilbert has proven useful on many levels. The paperback is the ideal mosquito swatter. My apartment in Lausanne is located right next to a forest, yet through an act of massive oversight, none of the windows has a screen. My choice is to either keep the windows closed, or deal with the mosquito invasion. Every night, before going to sleep, I grab *Eat. Pray. Love.* I walk from room to room, scanning the white walls and ceiling for buzzing activity. I stand quietly in the middle of the room. Very, very still. Only the faint sound of my breathing reverberates in my chest. I want the mosquitos to feel right at home. I wait for each flying bug to find a resting place on a flat wall. I take notice of how its hair-thin legs rub against each other. The way its minuscule eyes manage

to move in those tiny little sockets. Then, with absolute certainty, in one decisive swoop I squish it into a flat stain. Some turn into a black smudge, others into black and red. Once I've gone through all the rooms, I get a wet kitchen towel to wipe the mess off the walls. My book is the last thing I clean before I lie down to sleep. Strangely, I find this exercise meditative.

You will never believe this. I don't believe this. Guess what is graffitied right across the street from my apartment building in Lausanne? The word *Ismail* in Arabic. In white spray paint across a stone wall, somebody decided to leave that there to welcome me into my new abode. I don't know how to write Arabic, but I have seen my ex write down his name. I recognize the flowing shape of the cursive script that forms his name. This is a neighbourhood full of immigrants. Walking down the street, I hear many languages and see clothing articles that have clearly originated in faraway lands. Yes! I realize how ignorant I seem by not being more specific. My guess is that somebody decided to leave his own name on that wall as a way to say: "I exist" or "I was here". I wish that person knew they were sticking a dagger in my heart by reminding me of a name I have crossed an ocean to forget.

A thick sheet of glass separates me from Ismail. I can neither reach out to touch him nor avoid looking at him. He is always there.

Standing in the peripheral vision of my imagination. I wish to build a sturdy stone wall between us and put him behind it. Move forwards with my life. Leave him in my rear view mirror—but instead he is always standing there out of reach. Like a mirage. Taunting, never satisfying.

I remember visiting Ismail's family for the first time, in the small town of Morour in Morocco. Two weeks into our visit, one of the neighbours died and the wife, Sana, cried and wailed louder than an ambulance siren. She just ran outside her house and let it rip for all to hear and see. She was screaming, pulling her hair out, palming dirt from the road and smearing it on her face. I ran towards the window to have a look at what was happening. When I saw Sana flailing about right beneath the window I got scared. My whole body was shivering. Ismail ran towards me, almost anticipating my reaction. He held me on both sides, whispering into my ear: "Don't be afraid, this is what people do here." This is something I miss about married life. The way I had somebody who was responsible for comforting me whenever I felt distressed. I admire Sana's freedom in expressing her grief. I wish I could have an all out melt down as well. Just let it all hang out. Have a vibrant multicolor emotional explosion.

I remember when my father died. My mother and I held back tears. At the wake we kept assuring people that we were fine and politely thanked them for coming. The only display of emotion happened at night. I overheard my mother crying all alone in her bedroom. I had had my own private crying moments and then I went on with the business of getting on with life.

So here I am, lying in bed, staring at the white ceiling
thinking about that name sprayed across the street. I think it's time
for me to start my career as a graffiti artist. I will take matters into
my own hands. I will buy some paint. In the middle of the night I'll
paint over Ismail's name on the stone wall across from my building.
It will be a fantastic gesture of self possession.

Not all is horrible in my life in Lausanne. The transit system
does live up to my expectations. Not only are the buses, subways and
trains efficient, but they also run with such a high frequency I don't
need to plan my daily adventures in traffic. I simply stand at the bus
stop closest to my apartment building situated one black away from
the graffitied wall. A bus shows up within minutes and I am swept
away on a magical trip in this beautiful country. My favorite is riding
the trains and staring out the window. A bucolic scene of farms,
mountains and orchards passes by while I feast my eyes on their
beauty. The leather handbag that Sylvester gave me has proven most
useful on my travels. It's not too big to be cumbersome and not too
small to fit everything I need on my daily adventures. In it I carry a
bottle of water, a lunch of some sort, a printout of my heartbreak
recovery plan and a notebook to write down whatever insights I
have. Unfortunately, the insights have not been forthcoming. I have
realized that it's not riding the transit system that was triggering the

memories. It was hearing fragments of other people's interactions. In Switzerland, people are polite and courteous. They barely talk to each other. Even when they do, they speak in a foreign tongue. My insights notebook has remained empty since I arrived in this country.

I have discovered a bakery right across the street, behind the graffitied stone wall. It makes fresh apricot tarts. It has become my daily breakfast spot. French and German are the main languages of this country. Since I don't speak either one, I feel like a dummy wherever I go. This is a relief. I don't have to make an effort to communicate with anybody. I was starting to fear that I would forget how to speak. Luckily I met Claire at the bakery that makes the apricot tarts. Two days into my arrival in Switzerland, I saw her sitting at the table across from me. Our eyes met. A look of recognition passed between us. Two lost souls wasting time in a bakery. Claire has a smooth deep voice that comes out of beautiful lips. She is always impeccably dressed. Like a model about to go on a photoshoot. As luck would have it, she speaks English with a slight accent. She made the first move and asked me if I would like to have a bit of a chat. I meet her almost daily now. If it wasn't for my morning conversation over coffee with Claire I would spend the day completely mute. We have this unspoken agreement. We don't discuss what is ailing us in life. I didn't tell her about Ismail and she didn't tell me about who has broken her heart. One day Claire commented on my handbag. She touched it lightly and said: "That is a fine handbag." Claire clearly has an eye for fine fashion. One thing led to another. I told her how my bus buddy Sylvester had

broken my heart. Claire gave the most thoughtful comment. She said: "Perhaps Sylvester did love his wife. Perhaps he did mean every single word he said to you. He just didn't love her the way you imagined." Such wisdom. Her insight was comforting. I decided to believe her explanation.

Don't you wish life came with traffic signs? As you are about to proceed into a pothole a sign would show up to warn you about the danger ahead. For example, a big neon yellow yield sign could have sprung up each time I was about to say something mean to Ismail. Like that time I called him a fanatical moderate. His face contorted into twisty knots that registered levels of pain I wasn't used to witnessing. A message board flashing: "Beware of foot in mouth ahead!" before I told him that his social consciousness was putting a cramp into my lifestyle. A hot red "Dead End" sign before entering into an argument that neither one of us won. Maybe I wouldn't be lying in bed all alone in this foreign city wondering where I went wrong. But life doesn't come with clear signposted demarcations.

DeLorean

I HAD THIS MOST exhilarating, frightening and bizarre dream. I was walking towards a futuristic looking car in a multi-level parking lot. Somehow, I knew that I had just purchased the car. The car was a silver metallic color. It had a smooth round shape. I sat in the passenger seat. An electric panel stretched across the whole front of the car. Two minimalistic steering wheels were drawn on the panel. One in front of the passenger seat, and the other on the driver's seat. "Ah! You can drive the car from whichever side, cool!" I said to myself inside the dream. The brake and speed pedals looked like kitchen spatulas sticking out awkwardly. It was the only part of the car that didn't look futuristic at all, in fact looked like it was build by the cave man. I reached down below my seat to press on the lever that would give me more leg room. To my utter surprise the whole

car got longer and thinner. I was so comfy in my seat that I was worried I would fall asleep. My next challenge was figuring out how to turn on the engine. To the right side of the steering wheel diagram was a key hole. I looked to my left to the center console. Laid out in a neat row were several implements that looked like they might be keys. I picked up the one that looked like it was made from a tree branch. I tried to jam it into the keyhole. It wouldn't fit in. So I picked up the one that was made out of metal. Sparks flew when I got close to the keyhole and I screamed in horror as I dropped the key. I was feeling panicked and stupid. I can't even start the car, how am I supposed to drive it? Why did I buy this car? Then I picked up an implement that was made out of glass. That one did fit into the keyhole, but nothing happened to the car. I was forcing the key clockwise and anti clock wise, nothing. Nothing made a difference. Tears began to well up in my eyes, but before the water works could proceed in earnest, I had an idea. I dried my tears with my sleeve, reached over the glove compartment in front of the seat to my left and fished out the User's Manual. "Yes! Yes! Surely this will tell me how to start the car." Inside was an essay by former British Prime Minister, Tony Blair, explaining why he made the decision to join the US in its mission to invade Iraq in 2003. I read the whole ten-page manifesto, but there was no clue as to how to start my brand new car. Next in the User Manual was an essay by the Crown Prince of Saudi Arabia, Mohammad bin Salman bin Abdulaziz Al Saud. His essay emphasized the importance of modest dress for women while driving a car. I carefully read the whole thing, but nothing in there gave me a clue as to how to start my car. I

threw the User's Manual back into the glove compartment. What a nightmare. This must be the most useless user manual in the world. What would Antar do in this situation? And this had started as such a nice dream! I lay back in my super comfy and thin seat to stare at the car ceiling. The ceiling was white, fluffy and layered to resemble the grooves in the bark of an ancient tree. It was comforting. And then I had another idea. Maybe the keyhole is not what starts the car. This is a futuristic car, I need to think in a new way. Next to the keyhole was a rubber rectangle sticking out. It looked like a cigarette lighter, only it wasn't circular. I pried the rubber covering open. Inside was a hollow rectangular shaped tube with light emanating from its depths. I looked at the middle console to see if there was an implement that would fit into the newly discovered hole. There was a USB drive-like implement that had the same shape. I picked it up. As I placed it close to the hole, a natural magnetic suction pulled the implement towards the opening. The USB drive went in, in a slow steady speed that obscured the light emanating from its depth. The car's engine started and the front panel lit up. Yes! Yes! I had started the car. I had figured it out. And I didn't need the help of Tony Blair nor Mohammad bin Salman, lousy technical writers that they are. I pumped a fist into the air in victory and laced both hands on the flat steering wheel in front of me. The front panel looked like something from *Star Trek*. All the controls reacted to the lightest touch. I was able to drive the car. Nice and smooth. Driving the futuristic car felt so natural, It was as if the car fit me like a glove. Such a pleasant feeling. I drove down the spiraling parking lot, hoping to join street traffic. But then a

pedestrian walkaway appeared to my right. Since my car was thin, I thought: "I could fit through there. It's probably a short cut." As I approached the walkway the car automatically got thinner and longer and fit nicely through. To my utter panic there was a stairwell at the end of it. "Oh no! My brand new car will get smashed!" My palms started sweating, my breathing became fast. In my state I forgot to slam on the brakes. The car changed shape again. It got long and narrow. My body was gently rearranged into a standing position. On one wheel, the car smoothly navigated the stairs like a pro. The doors at the bottom of the stairs where pushed open to reveal an expansive football field. A group of teenagers were running around kicking a ball. I drove to the farthest part of the field and back in a figure 8, and then drove through a narrow alley and across the living room of a bewildered family. I finally stopped the car outside an apartment building. Why oh why did I take the short cut? This was so stressful. I was hyperventilating. The stink of my sweat was filling my nostrils. I was about to have a panic attack.

Out of nowhere my father opened the driver's door and sat in the seat next to me. "Go!" He commanded me. "Where?" I stuttered back. "Just Go! Take us where you need us to go."

I placed my hands flat on the control panel and was about to place my foot on the gas pedal but my father stopped me. "No, wait! Your brother is coming." Albert jumped into the back seat. The car expanded in both length and width to make room for all three of us. "Don't mind me, I am just coming for the ride," Albert said, lying across the back seat and closing his eyes, completely uninterested in what was about to happen. "Now!" my father yelled, and I started

driving. This time on the proper road next to other cars. It was all pleasant and relaxing.

But then Albert yelled: "Are we there yet?" and my father yelled: "No!" I swerved the car into a narrow alley to the left. I was really worried that I had scratched my brand new car but somehow the car didn't have a single dent in it. Albert screamed again: "Are we there yet?" my father yelled "No!" and I drove up a ramp and the car catapulted on the roof of a tall building. There was a gentle bump. I kept driving and feeling stressed. Why am I here? Where am I supposed to go?

Albert sat up and poked me on the shoulder: "Hey Car! Are we there yet?" My father yelled back at him: "Leave her alone! She can do it!" I drove the car from one building top to the next, leaping in mid air in between. It was an impressive display of driving skill. The cast of the movie *Fast and Furious* wish they could drive like this. For a second I thought: "Wow! I am actually a good driver."

And that is when I woke up. I was in my bed in my Lausanne apartment, gasping for air and drenched in sweat. A mixture of horror and pleasure was coming over me. It was the most mixed-signals dream I had ever had.

I was sitting in the bakery over an apricot tart contemplating the meaning of my dream. It's probably my anxiety at the graffiti I had painted on the stone wall across my street. It's very rare that I break the law. Breaking the law in a foreign country, especially one as law-abiding as Switzerland, somehow feels more exhilarating. I painted a bunch of colorful cars on top of the word Ismail in red, orange and yellow in childish strokes that would have looked perfectly suitable in a kindergarten. Luckily nobody saw me. I got away with my crime like The Pink Panther. I was feeling generally badass when Claire joined me. Somehow, we got talking about the nature of heartbreak, but only in abstract terms, keeping with our tradition of not discussing anything personal.

"Oh yes! Heartbreak." I let out a sigh.

"Do you know what helps?" Claire asked, cocking her head to one side.

"What?" I looked her straight in the eyes.

"Pink tinted glasses." She winked her long black mascaraed eyelashes at me.

I snorted a laugh. Very unladylike of me.

"No, really," she said. "When the world is harsh I put on my pink tinted glasses for a day. I always feel better afterwards." Claire smiled with expertly lipsticked lips.

Then she dug her sunglasses out of her bright yellow leather Parada handbag. She handed them to me. "Here! Try mine for a few days. I guarantee you will be buying your own pair soon."

I held the expensive pair of sunglasses in my hand sceptically. "Thank you! I will let you know how it goes."

The world did seem different with Claire's glasses on. The sky took on a purplish color and looked stark. The walls of buildings looked closer, as if they were pressing against people passing by. People's faces seemed kinder and softer as if their skin was emitting a faint light. My favorite part was that all the cars looked neon in color. As if their metal was radioactive. Claire was a wise woman. I couldn't wait to share my findings with her.

Navigation

BRINGGG! Bringg! Bringgg! I sat up in my bed trying to recognize the sound. Was it a fire alarm? Was it the door bell? It took me a few seconds to realize that it was the phone ringing. Not my cell, but the landline in my apartment which I had never noticed until today. Since nobody has ever called me in this apartment I was sure that it was a wrong number. I picked up the phone and said hello. There was a man speaking French on the other side. I said: "I am sorry I don't speak French, and you probably have the wrong number." I hung up. The phone started ringing again, but this time the man was speaking English with a French accent. "Please don't hang up, this is important. I am detective inspector Lars Arno. Are you .... Car?"

Oh shit! Somebody saw me doing the graffiti and reported me to the police.

"Yes, this is she," I said in the smoothest voice I could muster.

"What is your full name?" Lars said over strange ringing noises in the background.

"Carmen Franka, but everybody calls me Car. What is this about?" My heart was pounding. My hands were sweating.

"No need for alarm. We would like to ask you a few questions," said Lars.

Shit! Shit! Shit! Is this the country where a man got flogged for scratching a car? No that was Singapore. I think Switzerland is the country where they are anal about something else. Was is chewing gum? Or littering? Or spitting on the ground? I can't remember now. I should've read the tourist guide more carefully. Doesn't matter. This is the country where they are anal about something or other. Now I am about to be buried in big pile of automobile refuse.

"Okay," I finally said. "Go ahead."

"No, no. We would like you to come to the police station." I could hear a woman's voice in the background as Lars was speaking to me.

"When?" I was near tears at this point. Full on panic.

"As soon as possible," Lars said and then shouted something in French to a voice in the background.

I took down the address, grabbed my handbag which had all my necessities in it and rushed out the door. No apricot tart for me this morning. I was a ball of nerves as I stood waiting at the bus

stop. As I looked down hill to watch the cars streaming by, I noticed that the traffic light had a pigeon roosting at the bottom of the opening to the red light. It had a little nest built and was sleeping comfortably as the light switched on and off behind it. It was probably attracted to the heat. This sight touched me. I am like that pigeon, trying to make myself comfortable in a seemingly impossible situation. By the time I boarded the bus, I was calmer. On my way to downtown Lausanne I had to take the subway and then another bus. By the time I arrived at the police station I had become nervous again. The sight of police cars and uniformed people coming and going had made me all jittery. "I wonder if I will be able to come out of here once I step inside," I thought. I walked past the glass doors into a hallway. My left leg started shaking. I placed my hand on my thigh trying to calm the nerves in my leg. When I looked up there was a handsome dark man wearing a finely tailored suit rushing past me. Our eyes met for a split second. My right leg started shaking. I was worried that I would fall. My breath was shallow. I willed myself to walk towards the reception.

An industrious looking man in uniform was behind the bullet-proof glass. When I told him my name he nodded his head: "Oh yes! They are waiting for you in room number two. Please come inside. I will buzz you through." This was not reassuring. Clearly, I am in big trouble if more than one person is anticipating me. Will I go to jail? Will I be deported? I don't think they flog people in Switzerland. Thank God I am not in Pakistan. At least the jails here are probably clean and have modern plumbing. Stupid, stupid Car. What on earth compelled you to spray paint in public? I hobbled

into a room that was furnished like a living room from an Ikea catalogue. There was a sofa, curtains and a coffee table. Inside stood a young white man. He had tattoos on his neck and knuckles. His leather vest had fringes sticking out the side. His midriff was sporting a brass buckle with an engraved eagle. This is not how I imagined Lars Arno when I spoke to him on the phone. Next to him stood a beautiful platinum blonde woman. She was wearing plain jeans, a white t-shirt and a brown jacket. Her straight hair was held in a neat ponytail. She wore no makeup except for pink shimmery lip gloss. As I opened my mouth to introduce myself, the woman raised her arm, holding a picture right in front of my face: "Do you know this woman?" She asked. I gasped. It was a picture of Claire. Only she looked pale. Very pale. Oh no! I think she is dead. Is that a hole in her temple? My legs lost their strength. The room started swimming around me. I could feel myself falling but couldn't stop myself. "I hope I don't bang my head on that coffee table" I thought as gravity did its dirty business.

Two arms held me up and carried me over to the sofa. I looked up and saw the face of the dark man that I had noticed a few seconds earlier in the hallway. I heard him yelling something in French. After that I saw a great darkness hovering in the sky.

When I came out of the great darkness, I heard lots of yelling in French. It was mostly one man speaking aggressively and two others saying "Oui, commandant." Repeatedly. I opened my eyes to find myself lying on the couch. I placed my palm on my forehead to check if my head was still where I expected it to be. I had never felt so happy at the idea that my head was attached to my neck. The

yelling stopped. The man spoke to me in a soothing voice. "Ms. Franka, take it easy. You had a bit of a shock."

"Are you Lars?" I asked.

"No I am chief commander Rani Malik. Inspector Lars Arno is to my right over there. To my left is inspector Lara Yoder."

Rani gave instructions to both Lars and Lara and they both scurried outside the room.

"I take it you are their boss," I whispered.

"You guess right." He smiled.

"I must be in lots of trouble if the chief commander is talking to me."

"Don't worry about that right now. Just calm down," he said in a gravely voice while holding my elbow to help me sit up.

A few minutes later Lars rushed in with a glass of water and a cup of coffee. Lara followed him with a donut on a paper plate. I wanted to make some funny joke about cops and donuts but couldn't think of anything witty. The sugar streaming through my veins gave me a rush of energy. I exhaled.

"Chief commander ..." I started to say.

"Only they have to call me that. Please call me Rani."

"The picture I was shown earlier, was that Claire?" I was hoping my eyes had fooled me earlier.

"Yes we believe it's a woman named Claire Thomas," said Rani.

"She looks dead." I squeaked like a mouse. I had never heard myself sound like that before.

"Yes, that's correct." Rani nodded his head.

"What happened to her?" I asked

"We hoped you could shed some light on that," said Rani, adjusted his silk tie.

"Me?" I pointed a half eaten donut at my chest.

And thus the interrogation started. I figured out that Claire had been murdered. Shot in the head. They wanted to know everything I knew about her. I told them about how I met Claire in a bakery that made apricot tarts.

"Can you specify the bakery please?" Asked Lars while writing into a notebook.

"I can't remember the name, but it's right across the street from my apartment," I said, after pausing to think.

"You went there everyday for three weeks and you can't remember the name of the bakery?" Lara raised her right eyebrow as she stared me down.

"It has a French sounding name," I explained.

"This is Lausanne, all the bakeries have a French name." Lara rolled her eyes like an emo teenager responding to her mother who was about to lecture her on safe sex.

When my answers didn't satisfy them, they started to ask me a bunch of questions about myself, what I was doing in Switzerland. Both Lars and Lara seemed suspicious about my stay in their beloved city. Lara in particular was sending me a negative vibe. Whenever the questions got too aggressive Rani would raise his hand, say something in French and Lars and Lara would back off. Finally, they told me that Claire had a new cell phone. It had a single phone number on it—mine. I explained that we had discussed

going to the theater together. I had given Claire my number so that we could coordinate the time and date. At one point in the interrogation I tried to be nice by commenting: "I am so impressed how well all of you speak English. This would be so much harder if we had to conduct it in French."

To which they seemed to take offense: "In Lausanne almost everybody speaks English," said Rani.

I countered: "Everywhere I go I hear people speak either French or German".

"They speak French or German to each other, but that doesn't mean people don't know English," Lara said. She seemed to enjoy making me feel stupid.

After three hours Lars said: "This all doesn't make sense. For no apparent reason you decided to come to Lausanne, where by accident you met Claire two weeks before she was murdered."

"Perhaps it doesn't make sense, but that doesn't mean it's not true." I noticed that I had donut crumbs on my shirt. How embarrassing! I wiped my shirt with both my hands until it looked clean again.

Lara exhaled as if she was fed up. "Fine! Let's assume that everything you told us is true. Help us believe you. Walk us through your thinking process that led you to decide to pack a suitcase and reside in an apartment in a neighborhood populated by recent immigrants half way around the world."

"It's kind of a long story. It has no bearing on the murder," I said, the palm of my hand open on the table between us.

"That's okay," said Lara. "I want to know the whole story with all the little details. I will happily listen to it even if it takes hours."

"Fine! I will tell you everything even though it's embarrassing, but I have one condition. You have to listen without interruption." My hand was wiping invisible dust particles off the table.

All three nodded their heads to agree to my terms.

I took a sip of water and began to tell them the story in the best way that I could, hoping that I was a convincing storyteller. Otherwise I was screwed.

Car's story

This business of searching for beauty is a dangerous one. There are many battles to be fought along this path. One gets weary after a long haul. I totally understand why people give up and choose instead to dwell in a place of misery, drowning in a sea of complaints. It is so much easier to give up. This has been a painful experience. My tale is one which will serve to caution you against attempting to open your heart to joy. "Do you think it is easy to be happy?" If it was so, then everybody would be happy. You must battle the dragon of dark thoughts and slay the monster of your inner critic. These are no ordinary beasts, these were blessed with a drink from the cup of immortality. The minute you kill one, it comes back in a new form. Your battle will only infuriate them into calling upon their friends. They play unfairly, and bring into the fight the dragons and monsters of other people around you. They start with your friends, then people you care about dearly and when things get desperate your family gets involved. Even the best warrior

gets exhausted. I am telling you. Don't believe all the snake oil peddlers out there. You know who I am talking about, the ones that tell you: "Live your best life", "Be the best version of yourself", "Live a life you love, "Don't worry be happy", "Follow your dreams" ... blah, blah, blah. Oh, it sounds so nice and dandy, why wouldn't you want to live your best life? "Sign me up for that!" you might innocently think to yourself, unaware of the dangers lurking right around the corner. But what all those shysters don't tell you is the price that you will pay in the process. It is a vicious conspiracy to make people believe in the power of positive thinking. What do you think happens to all the negative thinking when you begin having positive thoughts? Do you think they will just go away without a fight? Oh they come back alright, multiplied, fortified and pow! in your face. Where once they resided in muted tones in your subconscious, resistance only makes them show up in a dazzling multicolor rainbow in your daily awareness. And there is nothing to get you ready for that. Listen to my wise advice, take my story and be sure to avoid the path I have taken

I had a long talk with my mother after I separated from Ismail. My mother wanted an explanation. "What happened?" she exhaled the words like she was pleading during prayers. I spent over an hour going through my list of theories, illustrating each one with an example, or two, or three or more. I will not go into that list here, because it would bore you. Furthermore, there is no way for me to attempt to be objective in a matter that is so intertwined with the inner workings of my mind. God knows I have my own issues and I am not the easiest person to live with. I told her how Ismail used to

tell me stories to help me go to sleep. At the time I thought they were just a form of entertainment, but now that I am reflecting on it, I can see that Ismail was attempting to communicate a secret yearning which I failed to decipher. Here is an example of a story that Ismail told me one night.

The Story of Shy and Fat

Michael, my buddy at work, told me about the Israeli corporate lawyer he met when he lived in Tel-Aviv. The attorney's name was Shy Penis. Shy is a common Hebrew biblical name. Penis a prominent family name in Israel. Despite Michael's familiarity with Hebrew and Israeli name morphology, I couldn't get over how funny this guy's name was. We would play a game where Michael and I would imagine scenarios where Shy Penis travels to the US and gets into all sorts of jams on account of his name. Michael and I would roll on the floor laughing during our lunch break imagining Shy getting slapped across the face by women mistaking a mere introduction with a sexual overture. Shy getting fired from his job for producing his business card during a corporate meeting. Shy gets evicted from his apartment building when he places his name on the buzzer controls. Hopeless, Shy refuses to change his name out of some misplaced national pride. But then he discovers that his misunderstood name has a cachet in certain circles. Shy becomes the number one porno star in LA. *Shy penis rises. Shy no more. The DD that changed my name.* All garner a cult following. Pretty soon - "Oh Shy! Oh Shy! Oh Shy!" becomes a call to action of horny men all over the world.

The other day I was telling the story of Shy to Andre, my South African boss's boss. He beamed at me: "Do I have the right story for you!" "When I was back in Cape Town, I worked with a man called Kos Shuman. Both first name and last name are typical for an Afrikaner. One day, he had to travel to Israel for business. Everywhere he went people snickered at the mention of his name. At first he felt confused by the reaction, until a kind soul explained to him that his name means "fat cunt" in Hebrew."

Andre and I devised a new story. Fat Cunt and Shy Penis meet, instantly they become best friends. Shy is forced to live in the US while Fat is forced to stay in Israel. But they continue to correspond via email. With each indignity heaped on Shy's head, Fat responds with a more horrific story from his country of origin. When a woman slaps Shy's face in a bar, Fat tells him the story of how a drunk woman in Israel pointed at her privates in a bar at him. Shy feels grateful for the slap. When Shy is fired from his job, Fat writes to him about how in his job each time somebody stubs his toe, he yells a profanity but then looks towards Fat and starts laughing, transferring the pain from the injured toe to Fat's heart. Shy realizes that getting fired is more merciful. When Shy gets evicted from his apartment building, Fat writes to him about how in his building kids in the neighbourhood buzz him and yell "Fat Cunt! Open!" before they run away. Shy realizes that American kids are well mannered compared to Israeli kids. Instead of becoming the star of The DD that Changed my Name, Fat becomes a black belt in kickboxing instead and devotes himself to inspiring bullied kids to turn anger into meaningful aggression.

After years of correspondence, Shy decides to pen a hand-written letter to Fat to express something odd that has been happening within their friendship.

Dear Fat Cunt,

As I walk the streets of my beloved city of residence, I try to imagine you walking around yours. I see you in your fur coat, the many layers that cover you in the hot Middle Eastern days, I feel concern for your well-being. People pass you and disregard you. Others avoid you like genital warts but I pity you, love you and despise you. I pity you because I recognize your quiet yet heroic quest for fulfilment, a quest I see in that juicy pink opening which I am fascinated by. I have spent countless sleepless nights fantasizing about filling that hole. Like me, you are a symbol of human life on this earth since time immemorial. I continue my walk, nonchalantly, and buy myself a donut to forget about you, amazingly it reminds me of you, and that says that I can't stop loving you. I also despise you for denying the eventuality of our union. We share the same predicament, the same fate, and the shame that makes people want to cover us up. It makes both of us nervous about our place in society. One of us is soon to be bullied. You, perhaps, again. I, certainly, now that social norms are turning. You, with your eternal mystery. Me, in my obvious readiness.

What I really cherish, my dear friend, is the contradiction of us, a paradox which permits this impossible correspondence. You, seeking hard to rebel against a status quo that was enshrined in holy

books. Me, seeking hard to dive deep into all that is shallow, superstitious and entertaining. But who are we kidding, my dear Fat Cunt in the hairy robe and the pink pearls! We are both seeking the state of non-belonging. We are both aware and terrified of this oppressive world whose magnitude, gravity, and constant growth obliges us to ignore it and pretend that we are free of it though, one day, fatally, it will overcome us. Eventually it will drive all over us leaving behind painful muddy tire marks. I could assure you that there is no salvation, no resurrection, no afterlife, no stories passed down from our kind worth telling, especially now that robots are about to replace us the way self driving cars shall eliminate taxi drivers. Tragic! No? It hurts to say such things. Yes, all we are left with is this contradiction, it is the only resistance available to us. Here I am, a male member, begotten by Zeus, Ra, Hubal, and Gilgamesh, an adventurer who seeks to believe in a world of his own creation. Here you are, daughter of Isis, Aphrodite, Ishtar and Al-Uzza, exalted for your purity and self sacrifice. Yet you crave the material world despite its corrupting powers.

Forgive my belligerence, my snobbish attitude. But there is no single faith that satisfies my shallow quest for truth. I am like that teenager in the story *Life Of Pi*. I believe in three religions and yet all the intensified godly guidance leaves me lost in a grand ocean of confusion. Predictable acts of heresy consume us both.

I fantasize that, one day, by accident, I will encounter you in the street and pet your coat. I will insist you acknowledge me. You might run away, but I will chase after you. I shall kiss you and embrace you. And then we will both realize how repulsive that was.

To combine our temperaments would be like placing an eye over an eyebrow. To become one—what a cluster fuck, a massive highway pileup, a shallow act of physical sport. Our stories are both tales of expulsions and exclusions, and if we have each another, then who are we? We become nobodies.

There is no word that I despise and loathe more than the word union, there is no act I fear more than the embrace of the beloved. To belong is to meekly seek the sameness. To desire a submissive acceptance of self styled slavery. To belong is to gather, get bigger, stronger and harder, to invade and pillage and consume and rape. Some say that is my destiny. One which I refuse to accept.

I urge you to ignore me. Never acknowledge my presence. Avoid me like you would an STD, please make a pledge, and cross to the other side of the street if you ever see me coming. Let's not consummate this fatal desire. Oh, but I forgot to mention your blossoming rose...

Sincerely,

Shy Penis

*** end of story of Shy and Fat

Clearly he was communicating to me how painful it was for him to be an outsider. That I didn't understand him. I was and wasn't the Fat Cunt to his Shy Penis. At the time I laughed, thinking that it was a funny vulgar story. Do you see the tragedy? My mother listened patiently to my endless rambling as only a parent could. When I was finished she assured me that I was justified in feeling aggrieved. In fact, she frequently noticed problems between Ismail and me herself but didn't say anything for

fear of being accused of interference. She validated all my feelings of distress and bewilderment. And then she said: "But, Carmen, you have a strong personality. You are one tough woman. The toughest woman that I know. I wish I could be more like you. I don't know what advice to give you. I only know that you will get through this and be better and stronger for it."

You see what she was saying? The failure was entirely mine, and when it came knocking on my door is came with a capital F to compensate for all those years where its opinion was not considered. Failure, failure, failure, the word stung inside my mind. I might as well had worn a big scarlet F on my chest to indicate the state I was in and the proper shame I was experiencing about it. There is no way around it, divorce is a form of failure. As if one failure wasn't enough to break my heart. A whole bunch of them congregated together and decided to drop on top of my head in a luxurious shower that didn't want to end. A year and a few months after the breakup of my marriage I lost my job. Therefore I had to face the shame of being an unemployed person after ten years of satisfying employment. Added to my delightful situation was that my driving instructor was going through a mental breakdown of some sort and as if a switch was flicked, in his eyes, I turned from his favorite pupil to the source of all evil and the most stupid person in the world. That forced me to question my qualification in an area I deeply enjoyed. So now I was a failed wife and a failed woman, a failed driver sitting on top of a failed career. Wonderful! Just to complete the picture my cactus had died, furthermore I had no access to a car.

Instead of improving in my driving abilities I was deteriorating. I tried to run away from it all. I thought if I drowned myself in a new experience it would help me get away from the big F. I would shake the big dark cloud hovering over my head.

Suddenly, for the first time in my life, I had plenty of spare time so that the thundering echoes of failure could ricochet freely in an endless loop inside my rib cage. Oh, how I wished I could do what the author of *Eat. Pray. Love* had done and leave everything behind and go travelling for a year. Okay, I confess, I didn't actually read *Eat. Pray. Love.* Don't test me on the details. But I heard so much about it from my friends that I feel that I almost read it. It would have been such a relief to travel to Italy and spend time eating pistachio gelato. I don't think I would want to travel to India to spend months chanting in an ashram. Seems a bit intense for me. I wouldn't travel to Indonesia either. I decided instead to spend the whole year in Lausanne, riding the bus, riding the trains and riding the subway. Instead of gelato I found an apricot tart bakery. I thought I would write a book about the experience called *Eat Apricot Tarts and Ride the Bus*, or perhaps *Healing my Heartbreak on a Swiss Train*. Argh! These are terrible titles for a memoir. But I would think of something catchy. The book would go on to a top spot on the best seller list and I would make tons of money and live happily ever after, where I become the most renowned failed driver to ever get a driving license. This lovely fantasy was totally doable aside from one tiny itsy bitsy little hitch—I am not sure if I can write a whole book. Although I admire what Elizabeth Gilbert did, my

personal circumstances have so far prevented me from following in her footsteps. Every morning, for the last three weeks, I have woken up bright and early. Had an apricot tart and coffee for breakfast. Then proceeded to have an adventure in your lovely Swiss public transit system. Dear respected police officers. I have been to Geneva, Bern, Zurich, Lucerne and Basel. After each adventure I would go home and lay in bed and allow myself to fall apart after swatting some mosquitoes dead. The next morning, I would get up early, take a shower, pull myself together, put on my brave face and repeat the cycle. Then one day I met Claire. She had a lost look about her. Only she looked far more stylish and put together. We would have a little chat over coffee. I really enjoyed this encounter since it was my only conversation with another human I had all day. We both recognized the broken woman in each other and we both had an unspoken agreement that we didn't talk about the source of our heartbreak. Claire's friendship was comforting.

As I lay in bed all alone staring at the ceiling, day after day, awful feelings came. Sadness, loneliness, shame, guilt, regret and judgement. I lacked the strength to do what I had usually done in similar circumstances in the past. Fight, slam the door in their face, kick them out and move on with business as usual. And so I decided that I would do something else this time. I welcomed each feeling as an honored guest. I opened the door and welcomed it into my apartment. Made it a cup of coffee and sat down for a chat. I listened attentively to what it had to say. I sort of hoped that each

one of my visitors would eventually get tired of talking and move on to go visit somebody's else house.

I got married for the right reason. I was madly in love. Once married, I threw my heart and soul into it and sincerely did the best I knew to be a loving and faithful wife. I made lots of mistakes in the process, but I can genuinely say that I tried hard to do well on that front. Now I was faced with a new challenge—Let go well. Would I be able to achieve that?

And now, my only friend in this foreign place is dead. It's my fault. It's this dark cloud hanging over my head. I am cursed. Everything I touch turns to ash. So put me in jail. I am a miserable and wretched creature.

End of Car's story

And then I started sobbing uncontrollably. I went through a whole stack of tissues drying my rush hour of tears.

Speedometer

SEVEN HOURS at the police stationed left me drained. I was like a wrecked car ready for the scrap heap.

Lara offered to drive me home but Rani insisted that he would do it instead. He expertly drove down the highway at just the top edge of the speed limit.

"Do you always follow the law?" I asked, glancing at his hands expertly holding the steering wheel.

"That is my mission. To defend the law." He smiled while staring at the road.

"Now that I am a murder suspect I think I should hire a lawyer," I said.

"*Mais non*. You are not a suspect. You are a *temoin* — a witness." Rani tapped his right index finger while saying this.

"All the questioning into the deep recesses of my private life, I get the impression that you suspect me of something."

"Lars said that when he spoke to you on the phone your voice changed the minute he told you he was a detective inspector. He sensed that you were hiding something. In fact, he regretted not picking you up himself instead of waiting for you to come to us. He has a good radar for such things." He switched on the right turn signal.

"I did panic when he called me. I thought it was about the stupid graffiti." I said, clenching my hands together in my lap.

"What graffiti?" He took the right turn with such grace, I hardly felt the move.

"I spray painted some colorful cars across the street from my building." I was doing my best to stay still.

"You think a homicide detective would concern himself with graffiti?" Rani laughed a big hearty laugh revealing beautiful teeth.

"The homicide part was news to me," I said.

"*C'est marrant*. Lars will laugh when I tell him this," Rani said, chuckling.

"Lars seems odd, like he doesn't belong at the police station," I said. I hoped I hadn't crossed any red lines. I didn't know what a *marrant* was. Maybe it was like a warrant.

"Lars worked uncover for seven years in the organized crime unit. He had to look like a drug dealer. He is slowly shedding that identity." Rani shrugged. "He's a sharp detective though. How do you say it—A plus?"

"Do you have any theories on what happened to Claire?" I looked at him.

"Claire was married to a known drug dealer based in Badem. Govan Durec. Thanks to the information you gave us, it seems that she had left her husband."

"Is it possible that this Govan had something to do with her murder?" I said.

"Yes, of course it's possible." He shrugged his shoulders.

"Why all these terrifying tactics to shake me down for information if you believe I am innocent?" Anger piled up in my chest and came out in my voice.

"It's our job to suspect everybody." He gave me a brief glance.

"That was one of the most horrid experiences of my life. You put me through hell. I was convinced that I was about to spend the rest of my life in a Swiss prison eating slices of cheese with round holes in them."

"Carmen, *du calme*. I can't charge somebody with murder just because the victim had their phone number on their mobile. Some of the things you said made us suspicious, *c'est tout*. We have to investigate every lead." He snorted.

"Don't call me Carmen, please. My name is Car."

"Carmen is a beautiful name. It's an Arabic name. Did you know that?".

"It's Portuguese," I said.

"In Arabic, Carmen means a garden that is attached to an orchid," said Rani. "When the Arabs ruled Spain for nine centuries

they popularized certain names. *Sans doute* some of that influence traveled to Portugal."

What suspicious thing did I say during the interrogation?" I asked, putting my hand bag in my lap.

"Lara thought maybe that you were a bit jealous of Claire because of her expensive clothes," Rani said.

"I was jealous of Claire but it wasn't because of her clothes. I was jealous because of the grace and style she exuded. Like she could wear a potato sack and would still make it look classy. Even if I had all the designer clothes in the world, I would look sloppy. I can't believe that a wise woman like her married a drug dealer." I shifted in my seat.

Rani sighed.

"L'amour makes us all idiots." He said.

He parallel parked right in front of my building and looked at the wall across from us.

"So this is the beautiful graffiti you were talking about." He smiled.

I let the words hang in the air with no response. After a suitable pause I said:

"Thank you for the ride. *Merci.*" I undid my seat belt and opened the door to get out. My feet were out but the rest of me was still inside. I looked up at my apartment. "That's strange!"

"What?" Rani leaned towards me and looked up with me.

"Nothing. I just don't remember drawing the curtains in my living room. I always leave the windows and curtains open for air." I pointed in the direction of my window.

"Get in the car. Right now," he said, beckoning me inside the car. I complied.

He drove away and parked the car again, a few blocks away and radioed for backup.

Lars, Lara and three uniformed police officers showed up and ran into my apartment building. Lara radioed back to let Rani know that my apartment had been broken into. All my things were strewn around. "Will this hellish day ever end?" I thought. I started hyperventilating. Each breath dragged in like a choo choo train. I scrambled out of Rani's car to get some air. I undid the two top buttons on my shirt. "This isn't happening. This isn't happening." I kept repeating like a mantra. When I noticed that Lara was running out the building in my general direction, shouting things in French. She grabbed me by the collar of my shirt with both hands and slammed me against the car. The side mirror of the car hit me right in the kidney while the rest of my body arched back like a limp rag. "Ouch!" is all I managed to scream. Very eloquent of me ... I know.

"You skanky bitch! *Espèce de conne!* You can't fool me with your damsel in distress act." I must say I was impressed with her command of English profanity. I am sure in French her effect is that much more potent. Then she grabbed my hair and was about to bang my head against the hood of the car, when Rani's hands intermingled with hers and I could feel the grip of her fingers loosen against my scalp. I slid down the side of the car and plopped on the pavement on all fours like a dog. I could smell the concrete, the dirt and the asphalt of the nearby road. I hoped that was what rock bottom smelled like. "This is happening. This is really happening." I

could hear Rani shouting something in French and Lara screaming: "Flash your boobs some more, *pourquoi pas?*" Then she spit in the air in my direction. Lars ran behind her grabbed her with both hands while yelling something. Lifted her up in the air as she pedaled her legs, trying to free herself to no avail. He threw her into the passenger seat of the car and handcuffed her left hand to the inside roof handle. He jumped into the driver's seat and closed both doors. Lara looked furious. Lars had the palms of his hands up in the universal gesture of "Calm down!" Is there anything more aggravating than somebody saying "calm down" when you are angry? Rani helped me up from the ground and back into his car. At least I was able to breathe again. I felt a confusing buzz of anger and adrenaline. Rani handed me a bottle of water and a paper napkin.

"I am sorry for this behavior," he said. "But I must ask, did you take something from Claire?" he looked straight into my eyes.

"No!" I ejected the word with all the power in my body. It felt like giving birth.

"I suspect that whoever killed Claire thinks that you have something of importance that is connected to this," Rani explained.

I shook my head, breathless from my previous effort.

"Did Claire leave something in your apartment?"

"She never been to my apartment." I was finally catching my breath and able to speak normally.

I looked down to realize that I was guilty as charged. Flashing my boobs for everyone to see. Quickly, I buttoned up my shirt.

"I don't think it's safe for you here. I will arrange a residence for you. Go pack a bag with your things. I will have a room ready for

you as soon as possible." I took a deep breath as he reached for his cell phone.

I ran up to the apartment. Two uniformed policemen were inside rummaging through my things. I dashed into my bedroom. Threw some underwear into the handbag that Sylvester sent me. A tooth brush, a hair comb and flannel pyjamas. It's amazing all the things you can fit into a handbag.

Ten minutes later I was back in Rani's car being driven to an unknown destination.

"Usually a female police officer would stay with a female witness. But our only female detective is Lara, and I don't think you would want her to stay with you. *Ca n'ira pas,*" Rani said, checking the side view mirror and rear-view mirror.

"Thank you for that." I leaned my head against the window.

"*Voilà*—the building you will be staying at," Rani pointed a finger forward.

"Stay in the car," Rani said as he got out and walked over to the building. I saw a man dressed all in black, donning a motorcycle helmet, approach Rani. Suddenly there was a gun pointed at Rani's chest. Rani expertly jerked the man's hand to the side. A bullet was discharged but there was no one else around. The two men started punching each other. The gun was kicked across the pavement, all the way to the entrance of the building. The man clad in black wrestled Rani to the ground and was turning to grab the gun. I moved my ass into the driver's seat and started the car. I drove half a block down the street, and up onto the sidewalk. The car jumped twice as the wheels got over the curb. I smashed directly into the

black clad man before he reached the gun. I pinned him against the glass entrance door of the building. He was groaning in pain, letting out high pitched yelps. I backed up, then put the car in first and hit him gain. This time the glass door smashed and the black clad man was wiggling like a cockroach on top of all the broken glass. I put the gearshift into reverse—what luck I had learned to drive a stick shift!—and backed up onto the street where Rani was still on the ground holding his right side. I stretched across and opened the passenger door, screaming: "Get in!" Rani crawled towards the gun, placed it into his mouth and then crawled into the car. I put the car in gear and drove away as fast as possible.

Chase

"WE ARE BEING FOLLOWED," I said as we raced down a cobblestone street.

Rani flipped down the visor to have a look in the vanity mirror. "Two black Range Rovers," he said. "They mean to kill us both.".

"That escalated quickly!" My attempt at humor went over Rani's head. Probably the language barrier.

One of the Range Rovers took a sharp right and disappeared from my view. "They're gonna t-bone us at the big intersection ahead!" I screamed. Rani rolled down the window and said: "You drive, I shoot!"

The traffic light was yellow as I approached the intersection. I knew that obeying traffic laws in this instance would be a certain

death. The two cars in front of me were starting to slow down. I swerved left to an empty spot, clipping the front of a bright pink Fiat. "Sorry, sorry, sorry!" I screamed as I sped through the fresh red light. A blue Toyota appeared in front of me. I could see the face of the horrified driver. The moment seemed suspended in the air like a hot air balloon. The details of the other driver's face, looking at me in horror as he held a cell phone to his ear, were so clear it was like I could feel him breathing on me. I felt myself giving up. I was anticipating the sound of metal crunching upon metal. All would be lost. Death was certain. But then a switch flicked. I heard a hysterical woman's voice scream "No!" as I took a sharp right to avoid the blue Toyota. Before I had a chance to exhale in relief the black Range Rover tailgating us had hit him. "Sorry sorry sorry!" I said, a broken record. A pistachio green Nissan Juke materialized out of thin air on my right. I took a sharp left turn to avoid him as he desperately tried to apply the brakes. When will this cursed intersection be over already? Right behind the Juke was the second sinister black Rover, coming at us in full speed. Clearly the two Rovers were intending to sandwich us. Rani leaned out the window and began to shoot at their windshield. The bullets left cracks in the glass but did not go through. "Shoot at the wheels!" I yelled at him. That's when I heard sharp crackling sounds coming from the back of the car. A man wearing a black helmet was standing in the middle of the intersection shooting at our rear. "Bullet proof!" yelled Rani. Thankfully our car was bullet proof as well. The second black Range Rover swerved and rear ended the green Juke. For a brief moment I felt sadness descend on my heart when I saw the tail end of my

dream car buckle like an accordion. But who has time to dwell on heart break when you are running for your life? I plowed the police car through the intersection leaving behind a mess of honking metal.

"*Merde*! Where did you learn to drive like that?" This is the first time I had heard Rani curse. Even I knew what *merde* meant.

"Racist Dave taught me." I said, happy to hear a compliment.

"Racist Dave?" Rani's voice was hoarse.

"My driving instructor. He taught me everything I know." I was gripping the steering wheel so tightly my hands hurt.

"Why do you call him racist Dave?"

"He is mildly racist but in a golly gee adorable way," I said, loosening my grip on the steering wheel a bit.

"This is the first time I hear that there is an adorable way to be racist."

"Well! You know! Like, oh, who cares right now? What do I do next?" I glanced in the rear-view mirror to check that we weren't being followed.

"Let me think." Rani said after a pause.

"How did they find us? How did they know which building you planned to house me in?"

"There is probably a police leak. I don't know who to trust right now." Rani had both palms of his hands facing outwards in the universal "calm down" gesture.

"Should we go to the police station?" I said.

"No!" Rani shook his head. "I know this place. It's a motel outside of Lausanne. We will dump this car. Spend the night there.

Two blocks away from the motel there is a used car dealership. I will buy a used car tomorrow morning as soon as the place opens. Afterwards I will stash you somewhere safe that nobody knows about before I figure out how to deal with the rest of this mess." Rani swallowed after speaking, the hoarseness was gone from his voice.

Rani opened the window and threw his cell phone out of it. Then he picked up my handbag. He found my cellphone in there and threw it out the window as well. "Nobody can track us now," he said.

We hid the car by driving down a farm lane and leaving it behind a barn. We walked to a motel where Rani paid cash for a room. It was past 10 pm. I was totally exhausted. My internal battery was dead like a brain eating zombie. Luckily there were two beds in the room. I threw my handbag on the floor. I collapsed on the bed furthest from the window. Rani took out his gun to place it on the side table, before he went flat on his back.

"I didn't know you had a violent streak," said Rani with his eyes closed.

"I don't have a violent streak." I turned on my side to face him.

"You nearly killed that guy earlier." Rani raised his arm, and without looking at me pointed his index finger in my direction.

"You are welcome. I saved your life."

"You didn't have to smash into him twice. He was kaput after the first blow." He opened one eye to look at me.

"Is this your bruised fragile male ego speaking?" It was now my turn to point an index at him.

"*Quoi?* I don't have one." Rani opened both eyes and sat up facing me.

"You know," I said, "Back home in the office building where I worked there was a law office on the third floor. I would frequently meet these self-important gentlemen in their fine suits in the elevator or pass them by in the lobby. Over time their faces became familiar even though I didn't know any of them. The same way you recognize people on the bus when you always ride the same time. One day I was coming back from lunch. A mentally unstable man ran past me. I saw him approaching people while screaming: 'I am with the FBI, you are under arrest." Then running towards the next person screaming the same thing at him. Finally, he grabbed one of my office building mates, a middle-aged guy in a fine suit. He kept shaking him, insisting that he must come with him." I sat up.

"What did this man look like?" Asked Rani.

"Which? The man in the suit or the FBI wannabe?"

"The suit."

"He was a nondescript white dude. His only defining feature was the tailored grey suit." I paused to collect my thoughts so that I could continue the story.

"Mr. Suit looked bewildered. People passed him by and ignored the obvious distress in his eyes. He was looking around him: "Somebody please help me!" he was pleading. I stepped in and challenged Mr. FBI. "He is with me, you can let go." Mr. FBI looked confused. He stuttered: "But my orders are...." I interjected:

"Yes thank you! You did a good job. Well done! I will take over now." Mr. FBI let go of the man's collar and ran away. I sighed of relief. This was the best outcome possible. Mr. Suit walked away from me in a hurry without acknowledging me. No thank you. No smile. No nod. Nothing. As if I was his attacker. After that I would catch him deliberately avoiding me. He would not ride the elevator if I was on it. Once I caught him hiding behind a big marble column because I was passing by. I spent lots of time thinking about his strange reaction. I had stepped in to help him out when nobody else would. Why should he have a hostile attitude towards me? I came to the conclusion that his fragile male ego was bruised because a woman helped him out. Maybe you are having the same reaction right now." I raised my right eyebrow to emphasize my point.

"Ok, you are right. My—how do you say—ego—is bruised. You are the damsel in distress. In this scenario, I hoped that I would be the hero. It's a bit embarrassing that I was saved by you." Rani laid back on his bed to avoid my gaze.

"And I got dumped by my husband for a woman he didn't know. My female ego is still reeling from that one! We are both alive. Let's be grateful for that. To hell with ego." I lay back down facing the wall.

"To hell with ego." Rani repeated after me.

We both fell asleep.

Headlight

I WAS WOKEN up with Rani poking my side. I tried to protest, but he placed his finger on my lips instructing me to stay quiet. "Lock yourself in the toilet and don't come out until I tell you to." He was holding his gun in the other hand. I did as told. Fifteen minutes later, I heard Lara's voice in the room exchanging tense words with Rani. I finally got tired of waiting. I unlocked the door. "What is going on?" I said, as both stared at me. Obviously, I had cut whatever they were discussing short. Each looked at the other waiting for them to say something. Finally, the awkwardness got so unbearable that Lara interjected. "Fine! *J'exiplique.* I used to follow Rani before when he would bring women from the bar next door to this motel. *Mais oui!* I am pathetic. It was a dark phase in my life. *Rigolez alors.* Laugh. The man that Rani injured was a *gendarme*

from Vevey. He is unconscious in hospital. Lars is in the car outside. We want to help you out. No matter your plan." She spoke quickly as if somebody was timing her.

"I was the one who incapacitated the assassin at the city center," I said with both hands on my hips in an Antar-worthy stance.

"You!" Lara said, her mouth wide.

"Lars sent you in unarmed while he stayed in the car?" Rani said, preventing me from savouring the moment.

"*Tu sais, Rani,* men always hesitate *un petit moment* before shooting a woman. *C'est notre avantage.*" Lara shrugged her shoulders.

"How do we know we can trust you?" I asked, playing up my newfound badass self.

Lara ignored me and looked at Rani. "You have to trust somebody."

Rani sat on the edge of his bed. "She is right." He exhaled. Then he continued. "Tell Lars to hide his car. Dump both your mobiles. We are spending the night in this room. We are renting a car and will hide Carmen at a resort in Basel. Then the serious detective work begins." He sighed.

Lars and Lara came in a half hour later. Rani suggested that I share my bed with Lara and he would share a bed with Lars. I shook my head. "I would rather sleep in an idling car parked in a closed garage than sleep next to her." Lara volunteered to sleep on the floor in between the two beds. Lars said he would sleep in the chair.

The next morning the two men went to get us a new ride. Lara was lying on the bed. I knew I should've let her be but I couldn't. I felt an intense hatred towards this woman.

"What's the story between you and Rani?"

"That's not your affair," Lara said.

"My life is on the line. I have every right to know what is going on."

"Do you think it's normal that a commander of his status would be directly *impliqué* in a case like he is?" Lara sat up in her bed facing away from me. I could see her back.

"What do you mean? How would I know?" I sat up facing her.

"When you came into the police station, I was monitoring you on a screen. Rani turned around the second he saw you walk in. He ran after you. And you, like a Hollywood actress, you conveniently fainted into his arms. From the minute you arrived at the police station he has been acting weird. All attentive. Not allowing us to interrogate you properly.".

"I wouldn't talk about weird if I was stalking my boss's boss." I cocked my head to the side.

"At least I don't throw my boobs in a man's face just to get his attention." She turned around to face me.

"I was not trying to get Rani's attention!" I said. "I swore to myself I would never date another Moroccan man."

"Rani is not Moroccan, *imbecile*. His family is from Tunisia. He was born and raised in Switzerland. To your tiny little brain it might all seem the same. There is a huge difference." She made a

circular motion around the temple of her head to emphasize the smallness of my brain.

I threw a pillow at her face. She stood up, fuming with anger.

"You stupid bitch!" she said quietly and deliberately in her exquisite French accent.

I stood up and lunged, trying to punch her in the face, but she rolled across the bed to avoid me and jumped up on the other side of it. She stood up standing there like superwoman. Hands on hips, feet parted. A defiant superhero stance. I grabbed her right foot and bit into her calf muscle. Lara yelped in pain. "You are proving my point." She grabbed me by hair and lifted me up then head butted me. My vision went bleary. I could sense warm liquid oozing from my forehead. I was overcome with an animal like anger that I couldn't control. I pounced. She tripped over the chair that Lars had slept in and fell flat on her back on the carpet. I ended on top of her, and tried to grab both of her hands to pin her down. Magically she hooked her left foot around my neck and peeled me off like I was a dirty old Band Aid. I found myself sitting on my bum in surprise. Instinctively I lifted my hands up to protect myself. Lara grabbed my left arm and twisted it behind my back. "Aaaaaaaa!" I screamed. I tried to hit her in the stomach with my elbow. I could feel the force of my jabs hitting her midriff, but she wouldn't let go of my arm. She was applying the force of her whole body on to me to lay me flat on my stomach. The pain in my left shoulder and left hand was becoming unbearable. I stuck both feet on the frame of the bed to resist her. In that moment Rani and Lars walked into the room. Shock registered on their faces. Lars moved first to move

Lara away. Rani followed him to pick me up. I found myself being carried to a car. "My hand bag, I left my hand bag in the room!" I screamed. Rani stuck me in the driver's seat and ran back in to get the hand bag. Lara was placed behind the passenger seat. A few seconds later Rani jumped in next to me screaming: "Drive!"

I started the engine, placed my foot on the gas and drove onto the highway. Lars was yelling something in French at Lara. "*Elle m'a provoquée*—She started it," she said. Both Rani and Lars looked skeptical. "Is that true?" asked Rani. "Yes," I replied.

"She is a highly trained detective. She also happens to be the only woman on an all male squad which means she has to be twice as tough as everybody else. It's really stupid to get into a fight with her," said Rani.

"I think I handled myself okay." I sniffed the air while wiping away blood from my forehead with my sleeve.

"You are lucky I didn't snap your little bitch neck," said Lara.

"You are lucky I have to focus on driving right now," I snapped back.

"Enough! Both of you!" Rani raised his voice.

"Yes, Rani. Why is she driving?" Asked Lara.

"Let's clear the air by listening to a story. Carmen, tell us a story for the road." He turned to me.

I thought for a minute. "Well I have this super edgy story about Juha or Mullah Nasreddin that Ismail told ......"

"No!" Rani stopped me mid-sentence. "I don't want to hear another weird convoluted story from your ex. I want to hear a story from Carmen,"

"I don't really have a story, but I know a joke," I said after a pause.

"Ok tell us a joke." Lars said in his croaky voice.

"Why did the chicken cross the road?" I straightened my spine.

There was a pause in the car. They all looked at each other.

"Maybe the chicken knew that the road was dangerous and decided to cross anyway. Maybe the chicken was suicidal. The more I think about it the sadder I feel. Maybe the chicken wanted to get to the other side .... The after life. It knows it will end up as generic bland chicken fingers. For the chicken, life is not worth living," said Lars

"Or maybe it spent a life time observing an eagle. Admiring how it flew above the clouds. Wishing it could be the same. Finally, the chicken thought: *Merde!*" I will never be able to fly, but I have these legs that can walk. And walking is what I will do. In a moment of pure self empowerment, the chicken decides to cross the road not realizing how dangerous modern day traffic is. And pah! All it's dreams finished in one tragic moment," said Rani.

"Perhaps it's an adventurous chicken. All its life Esmeralda the chicken was told by it's mother: "Don't cross the road! It is dangerous." But in forbidden stories Esmeralda had heard about the wonders that lay on the other side of the road. The amusement park, the fancy deluxe chicken coop and the handsome mysterious rooster. Esmeralda wanted to experience all this for herself. And ...... you know what happens," said Lara.

"Maybe there is no particular reason. Do you always have a reason when you cross the road? Perhaps it wasn't feeling or thinking anything. It didn't experience a childhood trauma. It wasn't trying to make a statement of any kind. Or it crossed the road because it had never occurred to it not to. It crossed the road for the pure simple joy of it," said Lars.

"Or perhaps Esmeralda read *Animal Farm* by George Orwell. Felt outraged by the corruption of the societal power dynamic and decided to leave it all behind. It wanted to spring forth to create a better world," said Lara.

"Or maybe we are asking the wrong question," said Rani. "Perhaps there is no road. There is no chicken. There is only crossing. Continual energy particles moving about. Become one with the crossing."

"Or maybe Esmeralda was asked "Who came first? The chicken or the egg?" The question sent the chicken into an endless thought spiral. Crossing the road became the only answer," said Lars.

"Damn! I will never be able to get this stupid chicken out of my mind. Each time I am driving down the road, listening to my favorite tune. It's the stupid road crossing chicken I will imagine, " said Lara.

We all laughed. The buzz in the car changed.

"Fuck!" I yelled.

I hit the brakes and the car came to a screeching halt.

"Fuck! Fuck! Fuck!" I raised my hands up away from the steering wheel.

The red Toyota behind us nearly rear ended us. The driver honked at us and gestured rudely at me as he drove past.

"Fuck! I did take something from Claire," I said.

Rani's eyes opened wide. "What?" he yelled.

"I mean I didn't take it, she gave it to me." I turned to face him.

"What?" Yelled Lara.

"I mean she didn't give it to me, she only lent it to me." I looked over my shoulder at Lara.

"What?" Rani, Lars and Lara yelled in unison.

"Pink glasses. She lent me her pink tinted sun glasses to improve my outlook on life."

"Where are these glasses now?" Asked Lars.

"In my hand bag!"

"This is dangerous," said Rani. "We can't just stop in the middle of the road. Pull over."

I moved the car off onto the shoulder. Lara jumped out of the car and grabbed my hand bag from the floor of the passenger side and emptied all its contents onto the road right in front of our car. She snatched up the pink glasses and sat on the hood of the car, fiddling with them.

Wallet, tampons, mini tooth brush, chewing gum, a paper map, underwear, pyjamas, used paper napkins and an assortment of knick-knacks that can be considered garbage were strewn on the road. This was embarrassing. Pap smear level intrusive. Luckily nobody was paying attention to me as I collected the contents of my handbag to return them to the comfort of its dark depths. Rani and

Lars huddled around Lara as she expertly donned a pair of latex gloves and dismantled the sun glasses using implements she had produced from her back pocket. Within minutes she had separated the left arm. Then using thin tweezers she pulled out a thin plastic looking thingy. It resembled the finger grip section of a tooth brush handle. Cars whizzed past us. The doppler effect could be both felt physically and heard audibly. If you ever have any doubt about how powerful cars can be, just stand by the side of a busy highway and let the force of passing by cars wash over you. Who needs roller coasters when you can get the same sensation for free? The rest of my companions were oblivious to their surroundings and absorbed by the pink glasses. Lara lifted up the extracted object to get a better look at it. "This thing has a cap," she whispered. Carefully, she pulled on the object until a metal piece was revealed. All three exhaled. "It's a USB drive!" Yelled Lars. "It's a USB drive!" said Rani. "It's a USB drive," whispered Lara. I felt tempted to repeat the same thing to be part of the group. The words didn't come out. I just stood behind them holding my handbag against my chest. Then Lara separated the right arm from the frame and found a similar looking USB drive inserted in there. She placed the dismantled glasses in one plastic bag, the two USB drives in another and took off her latex gloves.

"*Voilà!*" She flashed the plastic bag with the drives in my face. "This must be the reason those people were trying to kill you." She looked as happy as a school girl wearing a new dress. She really did have a nice smile. Beautiful teeth. The "kill you" part made it difficult for me to share in her joy. I frowned into her blue eyes.

"Car! Be happy. We are closer to solving the case." Then she grabbed both my forearms and platted a kiss on my lips. I stepped back to get away from her, wiping my mouth on my sleeve. "Yuck!"

"You are not into women then?" Rani said, laughing.

"This is sexual harassment!" I continued to wipe my mouth and tongue in an exaggerated manner to register my disapproval.

Lara got back into her seat. "Come on! Hurry up. Let's get to Basel so that we can find out what's on these drives."

We all got into our seats and drove down the highway with a new-found purpose.

Jump Start

ONE DRIVE CONTAINED a database of all the corrupt police officers in Switzerland. The other, a database of all the criminals interested in hiring them. Govan (Claire's husband) had transitioned from the dangerous life of a drug dealer into the safer life of an information broker. He had built the equivalent of a dating site for criminals and corrupt police officers. It was far more lucrative and less dangerous. This was the perfect get rich scheme. He would facilitate the interaction between criminals and police officers looking for extra income in return for a percentage of the spoils. There was just one little problem. Govan cheated on his wife and he didn't take into consideration that her vengeance would destroy his world. She had stolen his database to ponder if she should give it to the police. Claire's mistake was that she had hesitated. Instead of

taking decisive action, she had rented an apartment in Lausanne to consider her options. Maybe like me, she thought she could win her husband's love, somehow.

I had to stay in Switzerland for three more months to testify in court. I was even awarded a medal for bravery at the end of it. Imagine me with a medal for bravery! Who would have guessed? I did accept the medal even though I feel that I don't deserve it. Everybody looked so happy giving it to me—the president of Switzerland, the chief of police and a whole bunch of dignitaries. Even Lara showed up and congratulated me. My picture was published in the Swiss newspapers holding up the medal and smiling. I couldn't read the articles since they are all written in either French or German but I was surprised with how good I looked in them. I kept the copy of *Le Matin* (The daily from Lausanne). I am on the front page and I look happy. Not just a little happy, or amused. I look over-the-top, outrageously happy. My hair is flying in the wind. I am holding up the medal next to my face in one hand and the other is pointing up towards the sky as if I am expecting something to descend into the palm of my hand from a cloud. But the most striking feature is my smile. I want to go home and show this picture to my mother. "See!" I will say to her while pointing at the black and white picture. "It's possible for me to be happy again." I guess facing an assassination attempt makes you realize how lucky you are to be alive.

The day after the ceremony, Rani came the apartment the police had arranged for me. He handed me my passport and

informed me that the travel ban had been lifted. We sat around the small white dining table. I made both of us a cup of coffee.

"I can't wait to return home," I said. It felt so good to finally have my passport between my hands again.

"I was hoping you would stay a bit longer and I would get a chance to know you personally," Said Rani. He took a sip from the coffee mug in front of him.

"I miss my mom. I never thought I would be saying that. I also miss my nephew. I miss being somewhere where I understand the language." I petted my passport like a long lost love.

"I sympathize with all this. The last three months must have been an ordeal for you. Still. I would like to ask you out for dinner. I couldn't do it earlier." Rani looked at me with his black eyes.

"Let me guess? It's against the rules." I smiled back at Rani.

"The police are not allowed to date a witness until the case is resolved." Rani didn't smile back.

"I feel tempted to say yes. But I better not," I said, staring at his hands. "I am leaving as soon as I can book a flight. There is no point in starting something."

"Is it because my parents are Tunisian?" Rani asked.

"I know I am supposed to assure you that that has nothing to do with it. But I am going to be honest with you. Yes, that is part of it. I don't want to be bridging the east-west cultural clash all on my lonesome. Most people think that they are better drivers that what they really are. Other people are bad drivers, but they are ok. That is why bad driving persists. It's the same thing with racism. Most would say that they are not racist. And yet it exists all around us.

Acknowledging it in oneself is painful. If there is anything I learned from my marriage, it's that 'love conquers all' is a lie. I had this picture about my marriage while I was in it. Now, in hindsight, I am seeing a different picture. I can see how I didn't stand up for myself. I see how I used my ex husband as a sharp stick to happily impale myself on. I also see how years of socialization in a white culture, with white parents and a white life has left me with unconscious prejudices. I am not talking about the obvious overt racism like the KKK. My racism is the subtle polite kind. The regular white Toyota sedan type. You don't notice it because it's everywhere. I also realize that Ismail was socialized by years of sexism. Despite his best intentions, he couldn't break free of the macho man role. I can see now how hard Ismail worked to bridge the gap between us. I can see now that he loved me as much as I loved him. Maybe more. But I also see that our marriage had to end. It took so much courage for him to make the first move." I placed my passport next to my coffee cup.

"Love might not conquer all, but it does conquer a whole lot," said Rani. "A massive mountain of things. Ismail, your ex, is clearly a smart man. He is right in his view and analysis of what is happening in the world. He is wrong in just one regard. *Une chose.* There is no hope in his way of thinking. No room for things to progress. Without hope you have nothing—*rien.*" Rani flicked invisible dirt off his fingertips as he said the word in French. "If you give yourself a chance to get to know me you will discover that a relationship could have a completely different dynamic." Rani slid his hand across the table to almost touch mine.

"I am running out of money," I said. "I must fly home, get a job, pass my driver's test and sort myself out. I am also done with making all the sacrifices in a relationship." I withdrew my hand, placing it in my lap.

"*D'accord,*" he said, which I knew meant "okay" in French. "In that case. I wish to ask you for permission to stay in touch after you leave. Perhaps we can exchange emails. It would leave me with a bit of hope."

"*D'accord,*" I said. "However, I don't promise anything." I looked him in the eyes.

"When are you planning to leave?"

"As soon as possible. However, I want to spend a day or two in Zurich. I feel that I haven't explored that city enough. I can fly home from there."

"In that case, I insist on driving you to Zurich. With all that luggage it will be difficult for you to travel by train."

"*Merci,* that's very kind." I smiled at him.

"*De rien,*" Rani said as he got out of his seat to leave.

On my last day in Lausanne, I left my copy of *Eat. Pray. Love.* on the bookshelf. Perhaps the next occupant will find value in reading it. Or maybe they will find it an effective mosquito swatter.

Brake

IT WAS TIME to head home. Some say that the best part about going away is the arriving home. Although I am happy to go back into a familiar territory a part of me feels sad. I ordered a taxi to take me to the Zurich airport at 6 am. The middle-aged man was standing outside his car waiting for me. "Good morning," he said while nodding his head in my direction. He picked up my suitcase and placed it in the boot of the car.

"To the airport. Right?" He asked while opening the door of his taxi.

"Yes, to the airport please." I slid into the back seat and watched him close the door and then sit in the driver's seat.

"I assume an international flight." He started the engine.

"Yes, international. Thank you!" I looked out the window and saw one of Zurich's red electrical trolleybuses pass us by. I will miss riding those.

"I hope your visit to Switzerland was pleasant." He drove off.

"It was a bit too eventful," I said.

"Well! I know all too well about an eventful life. I am Kurdish. Do you know where Kurdistan is?"

"No! Please tell me." We passed the central train station. A train was arriving. I will miss riding the trains in this country.

"It's in the Middle East. Kurdish people live in Iraq, Syria, Turkey and Iran. I am Syrian Kurdish. Kurdish people have been persecuted in all those countries." He said while navigating a right turn onto the highway.

"And now you live in Switzerland." I looked at the river Limmat from my window. How I will miss this sight.

"I have been lucky in life. I have been married for 30 years to the most beautiful woman in the world. She is more beautiful today than she was the day I met her. She is a yoga instructor, an avid reader and an all round fantastic person. My best friend in the world." He tilted his head to look into the side mirror.

A tear dropped from my left eye.

"Together we have a daughter and a son. My daughter is in university studying business. My son graduated two years ago and works in HR in a telecommunications company. Honestly, I couldn't ask for nicer or kinder people to be my children. This is all the doing of my wife. Who in addition to all her qualities is a brilliant mother." He accelerated.

A second tear fell, this time from the right eye. Strange! What is going on?

"Now that the kids have grown up and are independent, My wife and I are experiencing a second honeymoon. It's more beautiful than the first one." He sighed in contentment.

The full waterworks was gushing forth. I wiped the tears away with a paper napkin.

"I can see that you are a woman on the verge. You are standing right at the threshold of a doorway to a different way of being. All you need to do is take one last step to cross." His eyes met mine in the rear view mirror.

"How can you tell?" I looked past the windshield into the sky and saw an airplane landing. How I love riding airplanes!

"It is written all over your face. You have the glow of somebody whose luck is about to change." He handed me a paper tissue which he fished out of a box by his side.

"How do I take that one last step?" I wiped away the tears.

"Every night before going to sleep recite this statement three times: 'I suffered. I learned. I changed.' You are almost at your destination." He stopped his car at the international departures zone.

I was sobbing uncontrollably.

The driver took out my luggage. I paid him his fare, and then I handed him all the Swiss francs I had in my wallet. A 200 Swiss franc tip. A tip larger than the fare. The driver shook his head. "This is too much." He handed back the extra money. I shook my head back. "I want you to have it." I placed the money on the

ground, grabbed my suitcase, hugged the handbag that Sylvester gave me and ran away before he had a chance to say anything.

"Thank you for the perfect ride!" I yelled as I ran. "And no, I refuse to take the money back. No. No. No." My hand ached from the weight of the luggage. I applied force into my steps. From a distance it probably looked like I was carrying a feather. I screamed "No!" all the way to my gate.

Spoiler

NO!

No no no no no no no.

No more. Never again. Over and done with. Nee, nyet, laa, Lo, nein, non, nahi.

No is not the opposite of yes. It's a necessary companion to it. It's a gate keeper. If you can't say no then your yes is meaningless. No is a work of art. A skill. A handy tool you can place in your back pocket to display in a sticky situation. No is a muscle. The more you practice it, the stronger it becomes. No-no. The lateral head shake. An index finger swiping left and right like windshield wipers. The powerful economy of characters. No is not a four letter word. It rhymes with flow, willow and Mexico—a country I visited once, but have to visit a second time. All the best words contain N and O.

Born, novel, automaton, fiction and wrong. It's a sound that forces you to purse your lips together and eject a sound through a limiting tunnel towards a light at the end of it. Towards a bigger potential. It adds weight to words. Gives them gravitas. Think of all the "tion" words. Absolution, abortion, gestation, fascination. They don't sound nice but they imbue a meaning that is blunt and direct. No is the reverse of on. It's gets you on people's black list. On a track of your choosing. Onto a supercharged booster schedule. No is the steering wheel you grab with both hands and decide where you want to go. Practice with me. No, no, no, no no,

no, no no, no, no no, no, no no, no, no no, no, no no, no, no no,

no, no no, no, no no, no, no no, no, no no, no, no no, no, no no,

no, no no, no, no no, no, no no, no, no no, no, no no, no, no no,

no, no no, no, no no, no, no no, no, no no, no, no no, no, no no,

no, no no, no, no no, no, no no, no, no no, no, no no, no, no no,

no, no no, no, no no, no, no no, no, no no, no, no no, no, no no,

no, no no, no, no no, no, no no, no, no no, no, no no, no, no no,

no, no no, no, no no, no, no no, no, no no, no, no no, no, no no,

no, no no, no, no no, no, no no, no, no no, no, no no, no, no no,

no, no no, no, no no, no, no, no no, no, no no, no, no no, no, no

no, no, no no, no, no no, no, no no, no, no no, no, no no, no, no

no, no, no no, no, no no, no, no no, no, no no, no, no no, no, no

no, no, no no, no, no no, no, no no, no, no no, no, no no, no, no

no, no, no no, no, no no, no, no no, no, no no, no, no no, no, no

no, no, no no, no, no no, no, no no, no, no no, no, no no, no, no

no, no, no no, no, no no, no, no no, no, no no, no, no no, no, no

no, no, no no, no, no no, no, no no, no, no no, no, no no, no, no

no, no, no no, no, no no, no, no no, no, no no, no, no no, no, no

no, no, no no, no, no no, no, no no, no, no no, no, no, no no, no,

no no, no, no no, no, no no, no, no no, no, no no, no, no no, no,

no no, no, no no, no, no no, no, no no, no, no no, no, no no, no,

no no, no, no no, no, no no, no, no no, no, no no, no, no no, no,

no no, no, no no, no, no no, no, no no, no, no no, no, no no, no,

no no, no, no no, no, no no, no, no no, no, no no, no, no no, no,

no no, no, no no, no, no no, no, no no, no, no no, no, no no, no,

no no, no, no no, no, no no, no, no no, no, no no, no, no no, no,

no no, no, no no, no, no no, no, no no, no, no no, no, no no, no,

no no, no, no no, no, no no, no, no no, no, no no, no, no no, no,
no no, no, no.

N
O
O
O
O
O
O
O
O
O
O
O
O
O
O
O
O
O

The End

Multi Media Pack

To receive multi-media content (videos, stories, music, coloring pages and much more) related to this novel, subscribe to the Take The Highway mailing list here:

ihath.com/MailingList/?p=subscribe&id=6

About The Author

Elen Ghulam is an Iraqi-Canadian living in Vancouver B.C. She worked as a computer programmer for 18 years before turning to writing fiction. Telling stories to silicon chips proved to be easy, and so she graduated to amusing humans. She is a passionate blogger at www.ihath.com.

One Last Thing

If you enjoyed this book or found it useful I'd be very grateful if you'd post a short review on Amazon. Your support really does make a difference and I read all the reviews personally so I can get your feedback and make future novels even better.

Acknowledgements

To Mary Knapp Parlange I owe a debt of gratitude. She painstakingly edited this novel providing valuable feedback along the way. I was lucky to find an editor who speaks fluent English and French. To my delight, she added all the French expressions in the novel. Many thanks to my friend Kathryn Aberle who gave me permission to incorporate her personal story about riding a taxi driven by man with a cataract condition into my novel. To all the taxi drivers from all the around the world who have driven me over the years, thank you for the inspiration. To all the public transport passengers in my dear beloved city of Vancouver, I have dissolved into your sea of humanity and emerged with this novel. During the summer of 2014, I had the privilege of spending six weeks in Lausanne Switzerland. The impressively efficient Swiss public transit system has inspired parts of this novel. To my family: Malik, Alexandra, Marwan, Ibrahim, Rawan, Yarra and Yusuf—for your love and patience.

Made in the USA
Middletown, DE
21 March 2019